THE
FOREVER MAN

BOOK THREE: CLAN WAR

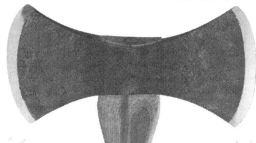

CRAIG ZERF

As always—to my wife, Polly and my son, Axel.
You chase the shadows from my soul.

Once I said to a scarecrow, "You must be
tired of standing in this lonely field."
And he said, "The joy of scaring
is a deep and lasting one, and I
never tire of it."
Said I, after a minute of
thought, "It is true; for I too
have known that joy."
Said he, "Only those who are
stuffed with straw can know it."
Then I left him, not knowing
whether he had
complimented or belittled
me.

Kahlil Gibran

CHAPTER 1

Marine Sergeant Nathaniel Hogan looked down from the hills of Drumnadochit and took in the view of Loch Ness. Above him the afternoon sky shimmered with the oily rainbow of the ever-present Northern lights. Next to him, also on horseback, sat Tad, the dwarvish muscleman, knife thrower, and astronomer.

Nathaniel pulled his fur cloak tight to combat the icy winds that swept the hills. Then he pointed east.

'Looks like smoke. Chimney perhaps.' Tad stared for a while. 'Maybe. Far away.' 'Shall we go and take a look?'

Tad nodded. 'May as well. Don't have any pressing appointments at the moment.'

They nudged their horses forward and started to amble in an easterly direction.

It had been almost eighteen months since the first solar pulse had struck the earth. One and a half years since the electromagnetic strikes, caused by a series of massive solar flares, had stilled the modern heart of mankind, and sent all of humanity spinning back into the dark ages. During those terrible months, almost nine tenths of the earth's population had died from disease, starvation, and sickness. In the United Kingdom over sixty million people.

But that is not all that had happened. The solar pulses had pumped out enough gamma radiation to affect much more than the simple electronic marvels of the modern world. The selfsame rays had caused a molecular level shift in Marine Sergeant Hogan's DNA and caused him to become a being of accelerated strength and abilities, the primary example being the capacity to heal himself from even the direst of injury, bar actual loss of limb or perhaps dread disease. To all intents and purposes, Nathaniel Hogan had become close to immortal.

He had become, The Forever Man.

As well as this, the gamma radiation had allowed a gateway between here and there to be opened and, through that gateway, a new civilization had come. Millions of them. Battle Orcs, goblins, and trolls—all commanded by The Fair-Folk, a race of alien creatures that were intent on leaving their dying planet and conquering earth as their very own.

By this stage, neither Nathaniel nor Tad had actually seen the Fair-Folk or their minions. However, they had been told of them as they had traveled north, something that the Marine needed to do, due to a geas[1] that had been laid upon him.

Before this, Nathaniel had magically traveled back in time to the era of the Celtic Picts and Romans and had been involved in a series of small battles against the Romans where he had led his tribe to victory.

Finally, some few weeks ago, he had

---

[1] an obligation or prohibition magically imposed on a person.

crossed Hadrian's Wall and then continued north, into the Scottish Highlands, where he now was.

As they got closer to the thin column of smoke it became apparent that it was indeed, the smoke from a chimney, rising straight into the frigid air. On approach, they saw that the cottage was part of a clachan or small hamlet of single story houses. The clachan was collected in a dip, nestled out of the direct winds and weather. A single main street and perhaps twenty houses. The road at each end of the clachan was barricaded by a stout wooden gate and a fence ran around the entire settlement. Nathaniel could see a couple of armed men standing at each gate.

'Shotguns,' said Tad.

The Marine nodded his agreement. 'Take it easy. We'll talk but not antagonize. Could do with a bit of warmth and a good meal.'

'I don't antagonize people,' argued Tad. 'You do.' 'Whatever,' said Nathaniel. 'All I'm saying is, if they make some crass comment about your height, just leave it. Turn the other cheek.'

Tad nodded. 'Will do.'

They approached the gate on the west side of the clachan and, when they were fifty feet or so away, they dismounted and continued on foot, leading their horses.

As they got closer the guards brought their shotguns up to port. Ready to fire at any time.

'Halt and state your business,' called out the one.

'No business,' replied Nathaniel. 'Simply two travelers seeking some shelter and a hot meal for the night. We have some game to trade.'

'Where are you from?'

'London. Been on the road for over a year now.' The two guards had a brief confab.

'Right,' said the same guard. 'Come forward and be welcomed.'

Nathaniel and Tad approached the gate and the guard pulled it open and let them through.

The four of them all shook hands.

'Go down the street, hitch your horses up outside the inn. That's the house with the smoke coming from the chimney.'

Nathaniel nodded his thanks. The guards stared at the unlikely pair as they walked down the street.

They tied the horses to the hitching rail and took their weapons, two shotguns, a crossbow, a selection of knives and Nathaniel's war-axe, from the saddlebags along with a sack of dressed hares. Then they entered the inn via the front door.

The door led into the taproom. The room was middling sized and warm. A huge inglenook on the left of the tavern was making a bad job of removing the smoke from the room but at least the fire burned well. A thick fug of wood smoke, stale alcohol and pipe smokers' herbs filled the room assailing all that entered. Forceful as a playground bully. A rough-hewn bar ran the length of the room. A selection of unmatched chairs and tables were scattered around, their lack of placement a true exercise in randomization. Perhaps a dozen men sat in groups. Talking softly. Drinking. Some smoked. Pipes or hand rolled cheroots.

Everyone stopped talking and stared at the two newcomers. Nathaniel and Tad approached the bar. Tad stacked their weapons up against the bar and the Marine placed his sack on the wooden top.

'Greetings,' said the Marine. 'We are looking for a place for the night and some hot food and drink. We grow weary of travel. We have this to trade.'

Nathaniel pulled out seven good-sized hares. They had been fully dressed and skinned and weighed in at around twelve pounds each. Enough meat to feed twenty-five to thirty people if combined with vegetables in a stew.

The landlord, a short wide man, balding hair, and thick eyeglasses prodded the game. Then he nodded.

'Room for the night. Dinner with meat, porridge for breakfast, and as much whisky as you want, within reason.'

Nathaniel nodded. It was a good deal.

'Thanks,' he said. 'Could we start with a couple of large whiskies then?'

The landlord took out two thick tumblers and half filled them with an amber liquid. Both Tad and Nathaniel raised their glasses to all in the room and took a sip.

The whisky was rough enough to bring unbidden tears to the Marine's eyes. Obviously home distilled. Young, raw, and fiery. But warm.

The two men went over to the fire and stood in front of it, letting the warmth seep in from the outside as the whisky took care of the inside. Nathaniel felt good. Relaxed and at ease for the first time in a few weeks.

And then someone spoke.

'Hey,' they said in a stage whisper, pitched loud enough for all to hear. 'Do you think that the lawn ornament has lost his pointy red hat?'

There was a sound of collective laughter and Nathaniel let out a sigh.

Tad shook his head. 'There's always got to be one,' he said as he stood up. 'That's a gnome, you moron,' the little man continued. 'I'm a dwarf.'

The joker sniggered. 'Where's your big red nose then?'

'And that's a clown. Really, are you the stupidest person on the planet or is your mother using the family brain cell tonight?'

The room went silent as Tad did the unthinkable and insulted a Scottish Highlander's mother.

'Damn you, dwarf,' said the joker. 'There's nae need to mention me mother. Time you were taught a lesson.'

'That might be true,' admitted Tad. 'But I can guarantee that the lesson will not be taught by someone as unbelievably thick as you.'

The joker pushed his chair back and stepped towards Tad. He was a large man, ample in girth but not running to fat. A body tempered hard by fieldwork and many hours outdoors.

Tad rolled his head on his neck to ease some of the stiffness out.

'Don't hurt him,' said Nathaniel.

The joker smiled. 'No worries, mon. I just want to teach the wee bugger a lesson or two.'

The Marine raised an eyebrow. 'I wasn't talking to you.'

The fight, if one could call it a fight, lasted all of four seconds. Tad dove to the ground, rolled, stood up alongside the joker and kicked him hard in the side of his knee, dropping him to the floor and then hooking him savagely on his temple, laying him out with one punch.

There was a stunned silence for a few seconds and then someone spoke.

'Hey,' they said, in a voice that sounded like a roll of thunder. 'You can't do that.'

Tad shrugged. 'I just did.'

'Yeah, well. You cheated.'

'Oh, pee off,' retaliated the small man. 'Is everyone in this village inbred or something? Can't a man just have a quiet drink?'

'They can,' rumbled the voice. 'But only if they're polite and don't beat up the locals.'

Tad rolled his head on his neck again. 'Alright,' he said. 'Let's get this over with. Take your best shot.'

The owner of the thunderous voice stood up.

And up.

And up some more.

He must have stood over seven feet tall and was built to boot. Most of his face was covered in a thick bushy black beard and his wavy hair fell past his shoulders. He wore a simple short-sleeved shirt, a tartan kilt and steel tipped boots.

He had muscles in places that normal people don't even have places.

Tad took one look, turned, and went and sat down next to Nathaniel.

'This one's yours,' he said. 'Good luck.'

The Marine sighed and stood up. 'Listen, my friend,' he addressed the big man. 'We don't want any trouble. Relax. Sit down. No worries.'

The big man walked over to the Marine and loomed over him. 'Too late for talk, wee man. Let's go outside and sort this out.'

Everyone in the tavern stood up and headed for the door, some stopped on the way and refilled their drinks from the bar. Nathaniel followed them all out and Tad brought up the rear.

The crowd formed a loose circle around Nathaniel and the Scotsman and waited.

The Marine swung his arms around in an effort to limber up. The big man simply stood, his arms by his side. Waiting.

Eventually he spoke. 'You ready?' Nathaniel nodded and moved forward.

The big man was fast. Faster than

Nathaniel would ever have believed. His massive fist struck the Marine in the center of his chest with a sound like an axe striking wood. The velocity of the blow lifted Nathaniel off his feet and threw him back, over the hitching rail and onto the snowy ground with a thump.

He rolled onto all fours and raised himself slowly to his feet. The world swam around him like it was on a gimble and the light faded from dark to gray and back. Without even feeling for it he knew that the big man had broken a couple of his ribs and, each time he drew a breath, pain shot through his torso.

He concentrated on pulling in energy from all around him, breathing deeply so that his ribs could knit, and his crushed muscles heal themselves. But he was concentrating so hard on healing that he didn't move fast enough to avoid the big man's next punch. A ham-sized fist cannoned into the side of the Marine's face, hammering him once more to the ground. Blood flowed freely from his split lip and, when he pushed his tongue against his teeth he could feel that many of them were loose.

'Hey, Nathaniel,' shouted Tad. 'Hurry up now. Its cold out here and my bollocks are closer to the snow than yours. Let's finish this before they freeze off.'

Tad's comment got a lighthearted cheer from the crowd and the dwarf bowed extravagantly.

Nathaniel shook his head, got to his feet, and took a few quick steps backwards to get out of the big man's range.

The massive Scot took another swing at the Marine, but this time Nathaniel was ready for it. He ducked inside the swing and tattooed the Scotsman's torso with a rapid-fire series of punches, delivered with sight defying speed. It sounded like a machine gun firing into a sand bag.

Nathaniel stepped back and waited for the big man to fall.

Instead the Scot grinned. 'Nice one,' he said. 'I think that I almost felt that. Next time put a bit more energy into it.'

And another humungous right-handed blow smashed Nathaniel onto the snow.

'Ouch,' said Tad, to no one in particular. 'Now that's going to leave a mark.'

There was another round of laughter and one of the watchers handed Tad a full glass of whisky that he accepted with thanks.

Nathaniel dragged himself upright again and stood facing the big Scot. It was now or never, he thought, knowing that if he didn't put the big man down in the next few seconds then, immortal, or not, he was going to have the proverbial bejesus kicked out of him.

The Marine circled the big man, flicking out a left jab every now and then, looking for an opening. Then he jagged back, moving faster than the big man could, spotted an opening and went in for the kill. Three solid blows to the big man's kidneys then he stepped back and circled again. This time he could see that he had done some damage. The big man took a few deep breaths but said nothing.

'What's wrong?' asked Nathaniel. 'No smart comments?'

The Scot swung another huge roundhouse at the Marine but, once again, Nathaniel stepped inside, slammed two more blows into the big man's kidneys and sprung away. Circling. Circling.

The Scot's face had gone pale and his breath was wheezing in and out as the pain from his beaten kidneys worked at his resistance. He lunged forward, attempting to grab hold of the Marine and get him into a bear hug. But Nathaniel dropped, rolled, and sprung up behind the Scot where he unleashed another barrage of blows at his exposed kidneys.

The big man grunted in pain and he shambled after the fast-moving Marine, throwing huge, slow punches that missed by feet.

And then Nathaniel moved again, stepping up close to the big man. He hit him once, twice, three times in the solar plexus and, as the giant fell forward, his chin met Nathaniel's fist coming the other way as the Marine launched the mother of all uppercuts.

There was a sound like a coconut being hit with a baseball. The big man's eyes rolled back into his head and he fell to the floor, unconscious.

There was a cheer from the crowd and someone pushed a full glass of whisky into Nathaniel's hand. He downed it in one go and it was immediately replaced with another.

Opposite him, the big man had risen up onto all fours as he struggled to stand. Nathaniel stepped forward and grabbed the Scot by his shoulder, helping him to his feet.

The big man gave the Marine a hug.

'Good fight,' he said. 'Never been beaten before. Can't say I rate the experience that highly.'

The Marine stuck out his hand. 'Nathaniel. Nathaniel Hogan, master sergeant, United States Marine Corps.'

The big man grasped the Marine's hand. 'My name's Gruff. Gruff McGunn.'

Tad walked over and handed the big man a glass of whisky.

'Good fight, he said. 'Most don't last more than a second against the Marine.' He stuck his hand out. 'Name's Cornelius Montgomery Thaddeus Parkinson. People call me Tad, for short, as it were.'

'Gruff.'

'Hmm,' exclaimed Tad. 'Good name—for a bear. I like it.'

'Let's go inside,' grunted the big man. 'Warmer.'

Everyone trooped back inside and started to do some serious drinking and eating.

CHAPTER 2

Commander Ammon stared out of the window of Saint Thomas' Tower that was situated above Traitors' Gate in the Tower of London. He took in a view that had been his for the last six months since he had claimed the Tower of London as the Fair-Folk headquarters and Saint Thomas' as his personal abode.

The river Thames was frozen over, and the white ice reflected back the multicolor Aurora Borealis as it coruscated across the sky.

Almost opposite the Tower a huge steel warship was anchored next to the bank, hemmed solid by the ice. Ammon wondered at the immensity of the structures that the humans had built before their crash. Although he had not traveled back and forth in time as had his chief mage, Seth, the mage had told him stories of wondrous things. Buildings that flew in the sky like birds. Carriages that were self-propelled through chemical reaction as opposed to magik. Weapons of such immense power that even the most dangerous of attack spells were as naught in comparison.

Also, he had told of wars without end. Wars that the entire population of the planet had been involved in. Seemingly meaningless conflicts where countless millions had died and then, afterwards, the same people all lived alongside one another, and traded and intermarried as if no war had ever happened.

Truly, the fall of mankind and the subsequent arrival of the Fair-Folk was the best thing to have ever happened to the humans, mused the commander. It was simply that they did not appreciate that fact yet.

And now, Ammon had called for a meeting of the council of twelve. He had decided that it was time to open a new chapter in the history of humanity. And this chapter would be titled, "The Reign of the Fair-Folk."

It was Ammon's plan to send many large battle groups of Orcs and goblins north to recon the area and begin to establish some sort of control in readiness for full occupation in the next few years.

He anticipated twenty groups of five thousand each. A total of one hundred thousand troops. The meeting of the council was a mere rubber stamp as he knew that they would agree. It was time that the humans were brought to heel.

CHAPTER 3

Axel had prepared himself for this moment since he had first heard the rumors about the Fair-Folk and their minions—the Orcs and the goblins. But the sight of the gray-skinned monstrosity, with its floppy nostril-flaps, bulbous head, savage mouth slit, and massive claws, was more of a shock than he could have imagined.

As were the two beings on either side of the Orc. Shorter, with large gummy eyes and grotesquely long, muscular arms. They were the goblin archers.

They had met on a field of clover a few hundred yards outside the walled abbey that housed many of the new town's three thousand strong population. Axel's mounted scouts had picked up the battle group a week prior to their arrival and the young captain had prepared for them.

Fresh stakes had been cut and laid in banks around the town. Rolls of barbed wire encircled the entire six-thousand acres of the settlement and every guard tower was manned by two men with crossbows and spears. The walls of the abbey were lined with catapults and giant scorpion crossbows, both the catapults and the bows loaded with bundles of loosely tied together arrows. When fired, the bundles would spread out and the enemy would be subjected to a hail of arrows. They had already been used twice in recent battles against large gangs of lowlifes and had proved to be deadly.

Behind Axel stood the entire five hundred strong cavalry, every one of them equipped with a lance, a shotgun with extra ammunition, and a sword or axe. Many were lightly armored with either military or police issue Kevlar body armor that had been picked up from surrounding towns and villages. They were a formidable force.

But they looked puny when compared with the five thousand plus troops arrayed before them. Three thousand battle Orcs, two thousand goblin archers, and even a small detachment of human cavalry, perhaps fifty mounted men. There also appeared to be some sort of large bear-like creatures at the back of the detachment. Shaggy fur and standing around ten feet tall.

Axel climbed down from his mount, adjusted his eye patch and stepped forward to greet the Orc commander.

'Hail, stranger,' said Axel as he saluted, right hand to forehead.

The Orc returned the salute 'Hail, I am Sergeant Neb,' he raised his right hand out in front of him slightly above head height, fist clenched. 'We come in peace,' he continued.

'Good,' responded Axel. 'Because we take short shrift with those who don't.'

'We seek information and trading rights with yourselves,' said the Orc. 'May we sit somewhere more private and parley?'

Axel nodded and turned to one of the

men behind him. 'Johnson, get the men to set up a tent here. Fetch Father O'Hara and the Prof. Also, water, some mugs and something to eat. Fruit maybe. Bread. A couple of legs of lamb from the kitchen. Not sure what these buggers eat so bring lots.'

Johnson nodded and trotted off.

Axel stood at ease and waited. Neither he nor the Orc spoke. It took a little over half an hour before the tent was raised and tables and chairs had been laid.

During the whole time both commanders said nothing. They merely looked at each other. Appraising.

The Orc sergeant saw a young thin skin. A livid scar ran down the right side of his face, slashing through his eye-socket and down to his neck. The socket was covered by a black leather patch.

His neck was thick with muscle, his shoulders were broad and his waist slim. He carried himself with the air of someone used to command. But there was something else. Something that perturbed the Orc. As a rule, Orcs did not feel fear, as such. They were bred to assess a situation in terms of strengths and weaknesses apropos a military viewpoint. And sergeant Neb could detect no weakness. Behind the young man's eye lay a wall of steel. This was not a man that one would cross lightly.

Axel was having a little more trouble assessing the Orc. The very alien character of the creature defied normal human appraisal. The captain saw a large thick-skinned animal bred for battle. A human pit bull or bull terrier. Massively built and obviously capable of fighting unarmed as well as armed. It was a formidable opponent. On the surface, Sergeant Neb seemed to be more of an order follower than a decision maker. However, Axel did not fall into the trap of relying on first impressions and assumptions. He knew of old that to assume would only make an ass out of U and Me.

He walked to the table and sat down, gesturing for the Orc to follow. Axel poured water and offered. The Orc accepted and then helped himself to a leg of lamb, ripping huge chunks off with his large canine-like teeth. Axel took an apple.

'What do I call you?' asked sergeant Neb. 'Axel is fine. Or Captain.'

The Orc nodded. 'Captain it shall be.'

Before Neb could continue there was a disturbance outside as two horses arrived. The two newcomers walked into the tent.

Axel stood up. 'Sergeant, let me introduce Father O'Hara, our priest and the Professor. Our leader.'

The Orc stood up and saluted with clenched fist. The Professor nodded. Father O'Hara crossed himself.

'Oh, faith and bejesus,' he exclaimed. 'Tis the divil himself come to visit.' He glanced outside the tent to take in the horde arrayed there. 'And with him his minions. six thousand at least be there, for he is legion, and they are many.' The priest turned to Axel. 'My son,' he said. 'I must beg forgiveness, but I cannot partake in a meeting with this heathen being. But mark my words, he is of the divil and no good will come of him. We must array ourselves against him at all costs.'

The father made the sign of the cross, strode from the tent, mounted up and left.

Axel raised an eyebrow. The professor shrugged.

Sergeant Neb did not react at all.

'Alright, Mister Neb,' said the prof. 'Talk to us. Tell us all. Where you hail from. Where you are going and what your plans are?'

Neb talked for an hour solid, his voice a droning monotone but his story was simple and to the point, told in military fashion with no embellishments. He went from the final days of the Fair-Folk's last world through their arrival, their expansion and right up to their current reconnaissance towards the north. He finished with a repeat of his assurance that they came in peace and they were simply on a fact-finding mission and wished to set up trade between themselves and any likely settlements.

'Look, Neb,' said Axel. 'I see no

reason to get complicated over this whole thing. Obviously, I have heard much of your leaders and I have already given this much thought. Neither of us wants a fight. If you are looking to trade then we are more than happy, but I see no need to tie up anything official. And, finally, I would appreciate it if you chaps would stay off our land. Easy to tell, ours is surrounded by barbed wire. If that's acceptable to you then I'm more than happy.'

The Orc sergeant stared at Axel for a while. 'We would like to leave a small presence here with you,' he said. 'To provide assistance if needed in case of attack by outlaws.'

Axel shook his head. 'No need, dear boy. We can take care of ourselves.'

'I have been instructed to insist,' replied the Orc.

The captain stood up. 'Well then I shall be compelled to reject your insistence.'

The Orc rose to his feet. 'I have been instructed to insist even if the use of force becomes necessary.'

The professor banged on the table to attract attention. 'Gentlemen,' he said. 'Sit down.'

The two warriors complied.

'Now, Mister Neb. Is it necessary to leave your, small presence, within our designated boundaries or will you be happy to place them outside?'

Neb thought for a while. 'Outside would be fine. But not too far away as then we would be unable to render assistance when and if necessary.'

'Right,' answered the prof. 'And how large would this small presence be?'

'One thousand troops.'

Axel jumped to his feet again, but the prof waved him back down.

'One thousand seems a little excessive,' said the prof.' I am sure that a token amount, say one hundred, would suffice.'

The Orc shook his head. 'Six hundred would be the bare minimum.'

'Two hundred?' countered the prof.

'Two hundred archers, one hundred battle Orcs, ten cavalry riders, and two trolls.'

'Trolls?' asked the prof.

'The big bear-type things,' answered Axel. 'Huge.'

The professor nodded. 'Acceptable, Mister Neb. Now, we are all busy people, Orcs, whatever. Let us be on our way. I ask only that you do not set up your encampment too close to the main gate and that you do not attempt to create a fortress. It would give the wrong impression. After all, we want peace, not war. Agreed?'

Sergeant Neb agreed, stood up, saluted once again, and left the tent.

'Sorry to butt in there, young Axel,' said the prof. 'But I could see that things were getting a little steamy. That … thing … is under orders and seems like there was no way that it could back down. We had to give it an out. What do you think would have happened if we refused?'

Axel shrugged. 'They would probably have attacked. We would have won. Probably.'

The prof nodded. 'I am sure that we would have. It would have cost us many lives but, ultimately, we would have carried the day. However, then what? What would we do when the next battle group came? Or maybe two, or five battle groups. Or a million of them? What then? We need to box smart, young fella. All is not as it seems. They bandy words like peace around, but it is obvious that they have decided on domination, and, quite frankly, as long as they do us no harm, I see no serious downside.'

Axel snorted. 'As long as they do us no harm.' He repeated. 'The only problem is,' he continued. 'They will be the conquerors. We shall be the conquered. That, in itself, is harm.'

The young, scar-faced captain strode from the tent and watched the legion of aliens march away. One hundred ranks of ten, swords riding high on their backs and bows shining in the sun.

And despite the warmth of the day, he shivered.

CHAPTER 4

Nathaniel peered through the foliage where they were hiding and stared in wonderment at the scene before him.

'Ugly,' he said

'Really ugly,' agreed Tad.

'Big and ugly,' continued Gruff.

'Oh, look who's talking,' quipped Tad. 'Mister big and ugly himself.'

'Bite me, dwarf.'

'And bite you very much right back,' responded Tad.

But there was no heat behind the exchange. It was merely two good friends insulting each other in the way that enemies would never be allowed to. Macho male bonding.

Nathaniel chuckled quietly to himself.

The bantering was comforting. It made the Marine feel like he was back in the corps. As opposed to being in the middle of nowhere, somewhere north of Hadrian's Wall in a world that was reliving the darkest period of its history. And, of course, now there were Orcs. And goblins. And some other big hairy monsters. Probably trolls or some crap like that, guessed the Marine. And there were lots of them. At least six thouand in this group alone, and it was the second such group that the three of them had seen in as many days.

This was reconnaissance in force, thought the Marine. However, until he had actually spoken to someone in charge they would not be able to glean what their mission was. Maybe they were peaceful. Maybe.

Nathaniel took another look at the legion. Took in their weapons, their demeanor, the way that they moved.

No, he thought to himself. No matter what these things might claim, they were hostiles. Maybe not yet, but … soon.

'Right,' he said as he stood up. 'No time like the present. I'm going in to talk to these ugly dudes. See what's up.' He unclipped the battle-axe from his belt and handed it to Tad. 'Keep hold of this. Stay here. If it all goes bad … well … I don't know. Come rescue me.'

Tad nodded. 'Will do.'

Gruff patted Nathaniel on the shoulder. 'Go get 'em, Nate. We'll watch.'

'Thanks,' said Nathaniel. 'I feel safer already.' He grinned and strode out towards the encampment. Holding his hands above his shoulders to show that he had no weapons.

***

Everyone from the clachan was crowded into the inn. Packed almost shoulder to shoulder, looking at Nathaniel who was standing on the bar. There was a general hubbub of noise until the Marine waved them to quiet.

'As you all know, Tad, Gruff, and I went to visit the pig-people, or Orcs as they call themselves, and their buddies this morning. I actually had a chat with their chief pig-thing and, I will say this up front—they are full of it! Now, first things first, they claim to have come from another time, place, planet, whatever. This, I am sure is true. They also claim that they come in peace and have no desire to either rule or to conquer humanity. I asked them why were they building a line of forts and barracks along the Wall of Hadrian? And why they were sending out recons in such force? Basically, whatever question I asked I got the same rote answer. We come in peace, we mean no harm and we simply want to trade. Our fortifications are here to protect you and blah and blah and so on. Now, I am a sergeant and I know officer speak when I hear it. Whatever they told me was simply what they had been instructed to tell me. However, I shall speak no more. I would like to introduce you to a newcomer who arrived with us last week. He has had previous dealings with these pig-folk and I want you to give him a listen. His name is Jarvis Baker and the Fair-Folk and their pig-people killed his father.'

A young man stood up on the bar. He looked nervous and held his head low, hands clasped in front of him.

'Speak, Jarvis,' said Nathaniel. 'No need to be afraid.'

'My name is Jarvis Baker,' he said, in a quiet voice. 'Almost a year ago now, the Fair-Folk ordered my father killed, and my uncle. My uncle was hung for sedition, he refused to bow down to the Fair-Folk, and my father went to his rescue but was cut down in the process. Before this happened, I myself rode with the Fair-Folk for a short while until we were issued with weapons. These were never weapons issued to be used on the Fair-Folk minions. They were not issued to subjugate Orcs and goblins. No. These were weapons to strike down other humans or, thin-skins, as they call us. After the murder of my father I left with my sister, Doris, my friend, Gerry and his brother, and parents. Following my father's instructions, we came north. And here we are.'

The young man raised his face and looked directly at everyone in the room.

'They have taken my father. They have taken my father's brother. And I have sworn revenge. There will be blood for blood!'

Tad leapt onto the bar, raised his hands, and shouted. 'Blood for blood.'

The rest of the room joined in, the chant an atavistic war cry. A tribal thing. It was the sound of the Highlanders seeking war. Looking for retribution.

'Blood for blood. Blood for blood. BLOOD FOR BLOOD!'

CHAPTER 5

Nathaniel literally ground his teeth together in frustration. He took a rough-rolled homegrown cigar out of his pocket, lit it, inhaled, and then exhaled slowly. 'Look,' he said. 'I'm not saying that we all gather together and simply attack the pig-people in some sort of demented rush. All that I'm saying is, we agree that we shouldn't let them past Hadrian's Wall, so we put together a border patrol, some fast reaction units. We know that they don't use cavalry and I am sure that all we need to do is show a spirited resistance to keep them out. After all, the buggers control the rest of England, so I honestly believe that a few bloody noses will discourage them enough to keep them out.'

A man with a long red beard and cropped red hair stood up. 'Aye, Marine,' he said. 'My name is Glen Cameron from Lochiel. Chief of the Camerons. I live in Achnacarry castle. I agree. But what I want to know is, when my men are patrolling the wall then who is protecting my stock and fields from the bloody Frasers?'

Another man stood up. Clean-shaven with dark hair that hung down his back. 'Screw you very much, Cameron. Like we would bother to steal your mangy cattle. Us Frasers have got some pride, you know. It's those Kinlochs that you should be worried about. They don't even have a chief. The clan is run by a woman.'

Yet another Highlander stood up and, without a word, walked over to Chief Angus Fraser and punched him in the mouth.

'Bite me, Angus bloody Fraser. I'll no have ye talking aboot me ma like dat.'

Nathaniel sprang in between the two men and forced them apart. 'Stop it,' he yelled. 'What is wrong with you people? We have a common enemy and still you won't pull together. Why?'

There was a silence in the room for a while and then Angus Fraser spoke. 'Look, mate. Not to be disrespectful; but who the hell made you chief of chiefs?'

'No one,' admitted the Marine.

'Good,' said Angus. 'Well bugger off then and leave the thinking to us chiefs.'

Nathaniel contemplated simply punching the crap out of all of them until they agreed with him, but he knew, deep down, that it wouldn't work. He was fighting against hundreds of years of inbred suspicion, hatred, and tradition. It was true that the Scots loved to fight. In fact, he had heard said that if you locked a Highlander in a room by himself then, within minutes his one hand would start to fight his other hand. And, while this was true, it did mean that they had a huge amount of internal disputes going on that seemed to be more important to them than the single overall strategy that Nathaniel was trying to sell them.

It also didn't help that the Marine himself was actually unsure of whether he was doing the correct thing. Who was he to decide that the Scots were going to be appointed as the guardians of humanity in the United Kingdom? Perhaps the chiefs were correct. Perhaps he should just bugger off and leave them alone to do their thing. No matter how stupid their thing turned out to be.

He beckoned to both Tad and Gruff and wandered outside, leaving the smoky confines of the room that they were in. He ambled into the nearby field and stood in front of the Clach a' Mheirlich, a megalithic standing stone that was carved with ancient Pictish symbols. He ran his hand over the carved serpents and the circles and wondered at their meanings. Marveling at the age of the thousand-year-old artifact.

Tad and Gruff stood close by. Neither spoke as they sensed that the Marine needed companionship but not company.

Nathaniel drew on his cigar, keeping it clenched between his teeth as he walked slowly around the stone, letting his fingers drag over the weatherworn surface. No historian had yet been able to translate the Pictish hieroglyphs and the Marine speculated as to what they said or meant.

He traced one of them. A circle, above it a flattened M, like a child's depiction of a bird in flight and next to it an upside-down T.

The sky above him coruscated with the oily colors of the solar flares and the cold air swept across the hills, ruffling the heather, and kicking up puffs of dried grass. Close by, a bolt of lightning flashed across the firmament and a clap of thunder rent the air.

The cigar fell from the Marine's mouth as his jaw dropped open in a revelation.

A Globe. Above it a Bird. Next to it, an upside-down T. An anchor.

An Eagle. A Globe of the World. And an Anchor.

Nathaniel started to laugh out loud. For, standing in front of him, carved one thousand years before—was the official emblem of the United States Marine

Corps.

Above him more lightning forked across the sky. The ground shook with peals of thunder. A whirlwind of rainbow color twisted down upon the Marine like a tornado of light.

And then—he was gone.

Tad and Gruff ran forward but the Marine was no more.

***

Nathaniel fell forward, striking his head on the standing stone as he did so. His vision blurred, and he shook his head to clear it. All around him the heather was now knee high. Above him the sky was the deep dark navy blue of early morning. A sliver of blood-red sun peeked over the horizon and there was no sign of the ever-present Aurora Borealis in the heavens.

He felt a pair of strong hands grasp him by his right shoulder.

'Are you all right, my lord?'

The Marine looked up. A large red-bearded man stood next to him. He was dressed in a great kilt, a rough spun white woolen tunic and leather sandals. On his back was sheathed a mighty broadsword.

Behind the large warrior stood a druid, dressed in traditional grubby white robes. Around his neck a bronze torc. His long beard was braided and adorned with the tiny bones of woodland creatures. Hanging from his ears were chains of gold and around his eyes he had smeared a mixture of charcoal and fat, giving him a look of dark lunacy. In his right hand he carried a bronze sickle, its blade dull with dried blood.

The Marine looked down and noted that he too was wearing a great kilt and sandals with leather greaves. He had no shirt and his torso was covered with a stiff bull-hide jerkin of hardened leather armor. On his left hip, a short sword. On his right, his axe.

He recognized neither the warrior nor the druid. But his shock was even greater when he turned around. Arrayed before him, forming a large ring, were over a thousand warriors. Standing still. And, in front of them all, another warrior, leaning on his massive broadsword, his beard fashioned into a club, tied tight so that it did not get in the way when he moved. A jagged scar ran down the side of his face, dragging the right side of his mouth down into a perpetual expression of distaste. He nodded at the Marine.

'It's time, highlander,' he said as he walked forward, swinging the sword back and forth to limber up his muscles.

The red-bearded man slapped Nathaniel on the back. 'Be strong, my lord. We know that you can win. Remember, beware his low strikes, keep moving, you're faster than him. Don't overextend.'

The druid stepped up to the Marine and slapped him across the face and back with a bushel of mistletoe, chanting as he did so. Then, he leaned forward and whispered into Nathaniel's ear.

'I am not sure if you are now him, lord. But, if the prophecies are true, then you are. If so, then I must warn you—you are not immortal here and now. Your speed, strength and agility are enhanced but if you die … you die. Please, lord, attempt not to do so. It would be very inconvenient to all involved. Now, step forth and fight for your right to rule.'

The druid gave Nathaniel a firm push between the shoulder blades and the Marine staggered into the circle formed by the mass of warriors.

Scarface swung a massive overhand strike at Nathaniel who barely managed to dodge to the side, still thoroughly discombobulated from his sudden transportation from one thousand years in the future.

The tribesmen were cheering and shouting encouragement. The noise was almost deafening, and it further added to the Marine's confusion. He shook his head again to clear his senses and stepped away from Scarface, rising up on his toes and dancing to the side like a boxer.

His antagonist swung again, and this

time Nathaniel danced easily out of the path of the massive blade, unclipping his axe from his belt as he did so. At the same time, he drew his knife and held it in his left hand.

The two men circled each other for a few seconds. Sizing up. Looking for a gap. Scarface faked a lunge, but Nathaniel didn't fall for it, instead bringing his axe in a low sweep towards Scarface's knees. Scarface jumped back and swung another overhand blow. Nathaniel swayed to the side, but the blade clipped his shoulder, slicing off a chunk of flesh as it did so. Blood sprayed high and a bolt of pain shot through the Marine's body.

He jabbed with the knife and felt the blade strike flesh, punching a shallow wound into Scarface's chest.

Again, they circled, both bleeding freely from their wounds. Scarface whipped his sword low, swinging at Nathaniel's ankles, but the Marine remembered Red-beard's warning and he jumped over the blade, moving forward as he did so. He grabbed Scarface by the back of his head and dragged him into a vicious head butt, smashing his nose and dropping him to the ground. But he was strong, and he rolled to the side and sprang up once again.

Nathaniel took the brief respite to concentrate his mind because, although he was fighting for his life, he had no real idea what was actually happening. The druid had mentioned something about the right to rule. But it was obvious that this was no ceremonial affair. This was a knock them down, chop them up, fight to the death.

The Marine pushed down any scruples that he had about killing someone that he didn't know or, seemingly, even have a real reason to fight. If this was his geas then so be it. He would fight to the best of his ability.

He raised himself up onto his feet and swung the axe around his head, jumping forward and sideways at the same time, bringing the deadly blade down on a forty-five-degree angle.

'Oorah!'

The blade bit deep into Scarface's left shoulder.

Nathaniel inverted the swing immediately, using his brute strength to drag the blade backward into a reverse cut that sliced across his adversary's chest, slashing through his leather jerkin, and exposing the white of his ribs below the severed flesh.

Scarface bellowed in pain and swung his broadsword at the Marine's head. A brutish overhead blow that would have cleaved Nathaniel in twain if it had connected.

But, once again, the Marine was not there. He had dropped and rolled to his left. Then, using a trick of combat that he had learned from Tad, he lashed out with his foot, catching Scarface in his knee. There was a crunch and the scarred warrior fell to the ground.

Nathaniel sprang up and raised his axe. He hesitated slightly at the apex of his swing, but the druid caught his eye and drew his finger across his throat in the internationally recognized kill sign.

The axe swung down.

Scarface was no more.

A thousand voices erupted in cheers as the warriors yelled their approbation.

Nathaniel sank to his knees. Pleased that he had survived. That he had won. But not happy that he had killed a fellow human being for reasons that he knew nothing about.

The druid walked over to him, pulled him to his feet and whipped him with the holly branch, chanting ancient spells as he did so.

Then hands grabbed the Marine and lifted him high and, in a procession of exaltation, they carried The Forever Man down the valley to the village of Ballyclyde.

CHAPTER 6

Nathaniel sat at the head of the table. On his right, the red-beard Scot who went by the name of Padan Fidach.

On his left sat the druid, Torkill Taggart, a name that literally translated as Thor's Priest.

Although the table was capable of seating twenty and the room was big enough for another hundred, the three of them sat alone.

'So,' said Nathaniel. 'Let me get this right. The man that I just defeated in single combat was Lord Sholto of clan Douglas?'

Torkill nodded.

'So, by dint of my victory I am now king of the Picts?'

Padan laughed.

'What's so funny?' enquired the Marine.

'Sorry, my lord,' responded the red-bearded warrior. 'I meant no offence. But, no, you are not king. By defeating Sholto in ritual combat you have taken over the right to rule his clan. Basically, those men that you saw outside. Half are yours and the other half were Sholto's. Now, they are all yours. However, they are only a quarter of the clan Douglas and there are also five more major clans and some twenty sub-clans such as Sholto ruled. There is only one king, Tavish MacDonell of clan Ranald, and he is not honor-bound to join against you in combat. The only way to make a claim to the kingdom is to rally sufficient swords to your banner and force a challenge from the presiding king.'

Nathaniel rubbed his eyes with the heels of his hands. Attempting to scrub away the utter exhaustion that was threatening to overcome him.

'Torkill.'

'My lord?'

'Who am I?'

The druid looked puzzled. 'I am afraid that I don't understand my lord's question.'

'Am I The Forever Man? Am I Lord Degeo?'

The druid nodded.

'Right. Then who was I before? You know, before I got here, before I appeared. Who was I?'

Again, the druid looked perplexed.

'You were you, my lord. You are always you. Who else could you be but yourself?'

'But I was somewhere else,' insisted Nathaniel. 'I was in the future from here. And then I arrived here just before the fight, but someone must have been in my body, this body, before I got here.'

The druid nodded. 'Yes, lord. Obviously. You were.'

'How?'

The druid shrugged. 'I know not, Lord

Degeo. You are The Forever Man. I am but a humble priest of the earth. You are the one doing all of these things not me. My knowledge comes solely from the prophecies and the stories foretold. I can repeat, I can observe, I can advise, however—I cannot be you, my lord.'

'All right then, priest of the earth, advise me. Why am I here?'

Torkill raised an eyebrow. 'Oh, that one's easy, my lord. You are here to do what you need to do.'

Nathaniel shook his head. 'Blasted priests. All the same. Riddles answered with more riddles. Padan, help me.'

The red-bearded man chuckled. 'The prophesies say that you are here to join the clans together. To forge them all into one so that you can wield them against the invaders and drive them from our lands.'

'Thanks,' said the Marine. 'Now then, who are our enemies?'

'Well,' said Padan. 'At the moment—the Roman Empire.'

CHAPTER 7

Marius Corcus was an Avocati in the tenth cohort of the Augusta the 2nd legion. As an Avocati he had served his allotted time in the Imperial Legions but, as he neither knew of, nor desired any other life beside that of a soldier, he had reenlisted. He had fought in both Germania and Hispania and had been awarded two gold armbands and a cup for valor. He had lost the cup somewhere in Hispania and had gambled the armbands away when he had first arrived in Britannia. But he loved his life in the legion.

He ranked high enough above the lowly Munifex so as to avoid manual labor and trivial tasks—as well as commanding twice the pay. But he did not rank as high as an Immunes, a rank that brought with it both responsibility and accountability.

He was the classic square peg in a square hole and he was happy for it.

Seated next to him on the communal toilet, his friend Avocati Seneca Lupus grunted and shook his head.

'You know,' he said. 'I haven't had a good crap since we arrived in this gods-forsaken land. It's all the barley that we have to eat. By Zeus, whoever thought that we would be forced to eat barley instead of wheat or oats? Bloody animal food it is. And it binds my gut up tighter than a drum it does.'

Marius chuckled. 'I don't have a problem. I've told you before, eat beets and drink a mouthful of castor oil every day.'

'All hail to the Cacator,' replied Seneca. 'The king of shits. No way am I swallowing that oil, nor shall I munch upon the flesh of the lowly beet. Barley is bad enough, darn horse food that it is, but beets are food fit only for pigs. I should rather suffer the pain of my plugged-up bowels than eat pig food and obnoxious oils.'

Marius wiped himself clean with a handful of moss, threw it into the waste bucket and stood up.

'Whatever, my friend,' he said. 'The Imperator has decided that we sally forth before the next watch to strike a punitive blow against the blue people in order to punish them for their last raid past the wall. So, make speed and join me at the gates. The tenth cohort marches alone under Pilus Prior, Marcus Albinus.'

By the time that Marius had got to the gates, Seneca was already right behind him. Both were fully kitted out with armor, kilt, helmet, hob-nailed sandals, and large shield. They also carried a pugio dagger, a gladius short sword, and a pilum, or heavy throwing spear. Both Marius and Seneca also carried a set of six plumbatae, long lead-weighted darts that could be thrown at least sixty feet and took the place of a light archer.

The tenth cohort formed up just inside the main gates, ranked into six blocks of eighty soldiers each.

Marcus Albinus, the Pilus Prior in command, rode on horseback at the front, flanked by two mounted centurions.

There was no speech, no call to arms, or talk of valor. The Picts were considered unworthy of such blandishments. The mighty Roman legions had been tasked with punishment and it was punishment that they would deliver.

The Imperator in charge of the legion had deliberately sent forth only a single cohort even though he knew that they would be outnumbered at least two, maybe three, to one. He did this with full knowledge that the Romans did not lose against tribesmen. He also knew that the news would travel. The tribesmen would know that many had lost against few. He was looking to humble as well as to punish.

They were proceeding to the nearby settlement of Badenyon. Home of around five thousand Picts including women and children. Ruled by Chief Morleo Drest.

The Imperator had no idea if Chief Drest's men were responsible for the cross-wall raid, but the settlement was well suited to Roman battle tactics. Situated in a slight vale and surrounded by flat, treeless ground, it would allow the free use of the tried and tested Roman formations against which the barbarians had no real answer.

The tenth cohort had been tasked with full victory. This meant that all would be put to the sword. Man, woman, and child. Even the cattle. The fields and the houses would be torched, and the men's heads would be displayed on stakes to further discourage anyone who felt like raiding into Roman controlled territory.

The cohort fell quickly into their stride and the centurions struck up their marching song.

I wanna be a legionnaire
I'm gonna shave off all my hair
Walk real stupid, talk real loud
I'm gonna make my mother proud

I wanna be a legionnaire
I'll wear a dress, but I don't care
An army camp is now my home
I'll kill and maim and rape for Rome
Scutum!
Pilum!
Sin, dex, sin, dex, Sin ... Sin Dex!

***

Young Connell came sprinting into the settlement, sandals slapping and kilt flapping as he did so.

'Romans!' he screamed. 'Romans coming from the south. Roman war party coming.'

The tribesmen reacted instantly. No time was wasted asking if the boy was sure, or how many Romans there were or even how far away they were. They all simply grabbed their swords and shields and spears and started running south.

The watch started blowing the watch-horn. A mournful *boo-ha* echoed across the vale, bringing yet more tribesmen in. Young and old they came, weapons ready. Hatred in their hearts and killing in their minds.

They stretched across the vale two thousand strong, in a line two hundred wide and ten deep. A numerical advantage of over four to one.

Chief Drest stood front and center, his two brothers stood one on each side.

'Why are they here?' asked Padraig, the youngest, only eighteen but as tall as a man.

'Why are the Romans anywhere?' replied Morleo. 'They have come to kill. To take what is not theirs by dint of force.'

'Well they've come to the wrong place then, haven't they, brother?' said Padraig. Youthful bravado attempting to drown out first-time-battle fear.

'Aye,' agreed Morleo. 'We shall make them pay for their arrogance. That is for sure.'

The Romans came over the hill in marching order. Within two hundred yards of the waiting tribesmen they deployed into a single line, 480 wide. Their movements precise. Parade ground perfect. Their shields shone bright in the weak Celtic sun and their uniforms showed blood-red against the green of the Pictish heather.

Chief Morleo Drest drew his sword from the scabbard that lay across his back and started to bang it against his shield. Slowly, all of his warriors picked up the cadence.

Then the pipers joined in. The asymmetrical wail of the bagless pipes cut across the valley and echoed off the far hills. Like a dirge of ages, raising the hackles on every Pictish neck as they cried for battle.

Standing across from the massed tribesmen, the Romans felt the first thrill of fear as the haunting sound enveloped them.

'Stand steady, men of Rome,'

commanded the Pilus Prior from his horse at the back of the Roman formation. 'Just a bit of folk music to get us in the mood.'

There was a rustle of laughter at the officer's joke and the tension ratcheted down a few notches.

As the pipes reached a crescendo the tribesmen charged.

'Mountain fall and field burn—hard are we and heather bred—Gyet! Gyet! Gyet!' shouted Chief Drest as they ran.

And his men shouted with him. 'Gyet! Gyet! Gyet!'

The Romans stood still.

Behind them the Pilus Prior shouted.

'Steady, men. Steady. Wait. Ready plumbatae.'

The legionnaires planted their shields in front of them and pulled a lead-weighted dart free.

'Ready,' shouted the Pilus Prior. 'On my mark, six darts rapid time.'

The tribesmen charged closer and

closer. When they got to about eighty feet away the Pilus Prior gave his order.

'Throw plumbatae. Go, go, go!'

Every dart was fitted with a small fluted hole so that it created a high-pitched whistle as it spun through the air. 480 darts whistled towards the target, followed closely by another 480. And another. And again. Again. Again. Almost three thousand screaming messengers of death dispatched in under six seconds.

Many missed their targets, thudding harmlessly into the turf. But many others struck home, embedding themselves deep into human flesh. Heads, shoulders, thighs, and feet. Fully two hundred tribesmen went down, slowing the charge and sucking the momentum out of it.

The Pilus Prior stood up in his stirrups.

'Men of Rome,' he bellowed. 'Form a wedge.'

The legionnaires rippled smoothly into a wedge formation. At the point of the arrowhead stood Marius and Seneca, the rest of the soldiers fanned out behind them.

'Double time,' screamed the Pilus Prior. 'Draw gladii. Charge!'

The Romans and the tribesmen met in the middle of the field with a sound like thunder. Over two thousand bodies smashing together at full sprint.

The Roman wedge cut through the tribesmen's formation with ease, splitting them into two separate units. The tribesmen fought back with great valor, crowding against the Romans, and swinging their massive swords overhand in an attempt to break up the arrowhead formation.

But the Romans kept their shields high and they fought like automatons.

One step forward, shield moved slightly to the left, gladius stabbing through to impale a tribesman. Shield wall closed. One step forward, repeat.

Romans in the middle of the wedge used their longer reaching pilium spears to thrust and slash at the enemies' heads and, when they stepped over the fallen, their small daggers were used to dispatch any who lay on the ground or, sometimes, the wounded were simply crushed under iron shod, hobnail sandals.

'To me,' shouted Chief Drest as he gathered his clansmen around him and charged once again at the iron wedge. But it was like trying to fight a stone wall. A stone wall that fought back.

The tribesmen were fighters, but they were not professional warriors. They were farmers and tinkers and craftsmen and thatchers. Brave men but, ultimately, amateurs.

The Roman legionnaires were full time, highly paid and trained professional soldiers. Many of the tenth cohort had joined up when they were fourteen years of age and had been fighting across Europe for over twenty or even thirty years. Their tactics had been forged against some of the hardest warriors in the world and, to date, the Romans had never lost a battle. Not a single one.

'Legionnaires,' commanded the Pilus

Prior. 'Form the saw.'

Again, the machinery of the Roman legion moved smoothly into place. The wedge unfolded into two lines of soldiers, the one staggered slightly behind the other, like the teeth of a saw.

The first rank crashed into the tiring clansmen, smashing them down with their shields and then stabbing with their gladii. After three or four beats of frantic fighting the Pilus Prior blew a whistle and the second rank stepped forward. Fresh arms and legs cleaving into the tribesmen while the first rank rested. After another three beats the whistle went again, and the ranks changed, forcing the clansmen back until they eventually broke and ran.

'Romans, close order.'

The cohort closed ranks to form a solid, tight packed line, shield to shield.

'Advance, double time.'

The line of Roman warriors crashed forward, sweeping away all before them as they jogged towards the Pictish settlement. By the time they got to the actual houses there was almost no resistance left. Behind them the field lay strewn with the dead and dying Picts.

The Romans had suffered only two casualties.

'Kill them all,' commanded the Pilus Prior. 'In the name of the emperor, leave nothing standing.'

The cohort broke into smaller groups, twos and threes. Almost immediately torches were lit, and thatch started burning.

The sound of women and children screaming in mortal terror rent the air as the Roman swords did their work.

Marius and Seneca smashed down a doorway and ran into a large hut. Lying on the floor was the bleeding body of Padraig Drest, the chief's youngest brother. Blood poured from a multitude of wounds. His stomach, his head, both arms. Around him stood a group of young children and, sitting on the floor, Padraig's head in her lap, sat a beautiful young girl. Probably fifteen years old. She was weeping.

Marius stepped forward and raised his

sword. A small boy jumped in front of him. He was holding Padraig's huge broadsword, but he could barely stand upright with the massive weight of steel in his hands. There was absolutely no chance of him actually raising the blade clear of the ground.

'Get back, Roman dog,' the boy shouted. 'Leave my uncle alone or face my wrath.'

'By Mars and Juno,' cursed Seneca. 'Just kill the little savage and let's get on with it.'

Marius moved towards the little boy and, as he did so, he noticed a dark stain spread across the front of the boy's trews as he wet himself in terror.

But he did not move as he strained to lift the mighty sword.

Outside the hut one of the centurions shouted. 'Marius. What's going on in there? Any occupants.'

Seneca was about to answer but Marius put his finger to his lips, signaling silence.

'Nothing here, centurion,' yelled Marius. 'Just checking for valuables.'

Seneca raised an eyebrow.

Marius shook his head. 'I don't kill women and children and dying men. Never have, never will.'

'Well get out of the way then,' said Seneca. 'Because I do.'

He raised his sword and brought it down on the boy's neck with enough force to separate his head from his scrawny shoulders.

But the blade never connected as Marius parried the blow and sent a reverse slash through Seneca's neck, severing his jugular and spilling his life's blood. Then he grabbed the body and dragged it outside, pulling it to the burning hut next door and throwing it into the flames before anyone noticed. Afterwards he ran to join up with the rest of the cohort as it started to reform.

The Romans drew up into their ranks, standing silent amongst the burning remains of the dead and dying settlement.

Once again, the imperial lion of Rome had bared its teeth.

With measured cadence they marched out. Heading home.

Lying bleeding, on the floor of one of the few remaining huts, the new young chief of the now decimated tribe lay broken and bleeding.

But he would not die. Because his hatred was keeping him alive.

And Chief Padraig Drest swore his revenge.

CHAPTER 8

Nathaniel grunted as Janiver pulled the stitches tight, sewing up the wound in his right shoulder muscle. The price of being a little too slow in his last fight.

He had won. Just as he had won the last five before. But he bore a number of scars from every encounter and he was in bad need of a protracted period of rest and recuperation.

Janiver leant forward and bit the length of gut off with her teeth, tucking and tying the loose end, packing it with a paste of boiled down cow's urine and then wrapping a clean linen bandage around the wound. Then she produced a comb and combed the knots out of his long dark hair, finally plaiting it so that it lay down his back, between his shoulder blades. Then she did the same to his beard, combing it and plaiting it and winding it with threads of golden wire.

Her administrations complete, she kissed him tenderly on the lips and took his face in her hands and stared into his eyes.

'My lord, Arnthor,' she said. 'I wish that you could stop fighting. My heart stops at the thought of losing you.'

Nathaniel grinned. He had been introduced to the beautiful Pictish woman a mere few days after he had arrived, and he had immediately felt a close rapport. As if he had known her for years. When he told this to Torkill the druid, the priest had nodded sagely and then told Nathaniel that he had actually known Janiver for many years.

When the Marine had asked how this was possible Torkill, had told him that he was The Forever Man. He had always, and would always have known, and loved Janiver. It was both ordained and preordained. Again, Nathaniel had asked how, but Torkill had merely shrugged in that maddening way of his and told the Marine that he had no idea, he was merely a priest of the Earth and Nathaniel was The Forever Man.

Eventually Nathaniel had given up trying to puzzle out the when's and why's and he had simply reveled in Janiver's obvious love and hero-worship.

'Fear not, my darling,' he said. 'For am I not The Forever Man?'

She nodded. 'That is why I call you Arnthor, chosen by Thor, for you truly do sit on the right hand of the father of all gods. But even gods can die.'

The Marine kissed her. 'Bring me my great kilt, woman,' he said. 'Enough talk of death. Tonight, we rejoice, for I have gained control of another clan. I now control six. Not long and I shall be in a position to challenge Tavish MacDonell of clan Ranald for the kingship. Then, once I have united all of the clans, we can concentrate on doing what I am destined to do—fight the Romans.'

Janiver helped him on with his kilt,

pleating the bottom half and belting it around his waist then hanging the plaid by draping the top half of the material over his left shoulder and tying it to his belt. Nathaniel's kilt was made up of strips of tartan from all of the clans that he had thus far conquered. A garish mix of reds and blues, green and yellows.

His axe went onto the right-hand side of his belt, a short sword on his left, a dagger into a sheath on his left calf and another small throwing knife on a thong around his neck.

Janiver wore a white, floor-length linen dress, simple and formfitting. Around her waist, a thin gold chain.

No jewelry apart from a band of gold around her head, almost, but not quite, a tiara.

They left the main hut and walked to the feasting area accompanied by the druid, Torkill and Nathaniel's right-hand man, the red-bearded Padan.

When they reached the area, they were greeted by a huge cheer. Nathaniel smiled and sat at his appointed seat, the head of the main table. But Janiver stayed on her feet and wandered amongst the crowd for a while. Greeting, talking, resting her hands on some men's shoulders. And wherever she went the sense of love and worship for her was an almost palpable thing. For, if Nathaniel was both their leader, and The Forever Man—he was untouchable. Aloof. Almost a god. But Janiver was theirs. A woman of flesh and blood. Born of a known family and grown up in the highlands. She was their link between the mundane humanity of their own existence and the otherworldly existence of The Forever Man. A man that even the druids held in awe.

'She assumes too much,' whispered Torkill to Padan. 'She is not yet queen but she acts as such.'

Padan shrugged. 'So? The people love her. Let her have her fun, she works hard and receives little enough attention from Lord Degeo who has too few hours in the day to achieve all that he needs to.'

The druid noted well the look in

Padan's eyes, seeing in him the same adoration that he saw in the crowd and he ceased speaking. It would do no good, he thought. The woman had cast a spell on them all, not a literal one, of course, but a binding one nevertheless. He could not be affected as he was a druid and, as such, was also celibate. Mother earth was his lover and father, Thor was his belief. But it mattered not, he concluded. Padan was correct, the people loved her and, the people were Nathaniel's people so, ipso facto—the people loved Nathaniel.

The festivities went on late into the night and Nathaniel worked the crowd, talking to all, cajoling, discussing and simply inveigling himself. He tried to steal the odd moment with Janiver, but such were the many demands on him that he saw her only from a distance throughout the entire evening.

As the night progressed, oxen were roasted on a spit and heaping piles of vegetables, loaves of fresh baked bread, and gallons of mead and ale were served up to all. Dances were danced, and songs were sung, and, when the sun rose, Torkill sacrificed a goat and called on Thor's blessing to all.

Eventually Janiver retired to the bedchamber and, after she had left, the festivities drew to a close. But Nathaniel stayed on with a select group of chiefs, discussing the future and planning his next steps until the first sliver of morning sun peeked clear of the horizon and led him to bed.

Later that next day a small group of people arrived at Nathaniel's settlement. Ten women and children surrounded four old men who were carrying a bier. And, on the stretcher lay Padraig Drest. His face was drawn in agony and his skin was as pale as death—but he still lived, born aloft by his desire for revenge and his hatred of the Romans.

Nathaniel came out to see him and the young man grasped the Marine by his hand and, his story interrupted by his blood-gurgling breathlessness, he told Nathaniel of the attack on his settlement. Of the killing of his brothers and all of his people.

The merciless slaying of women and children. And then he swore his obedience to The Forever Man.

'I have no tribe left to speak of,' he whispered. 'But my family is large and powerful. As soon as I have regained my strength I will ensure that at least another three tribes flock to your banner. The time for clan warfare is over. It is time to fight the Romans and only the Romans.'

Nathaniel nodded. He turned to the druid.

'Take this man to my living quarters,' he commanded. 'Make sure that he lives and that he has all that he needs. Treat him as you would my son.'

Torkill bowed deeply. 'As you wish, my lord.'

The Marine beckoned to Janiver. 'Go with. Check his wounds, see that he is fed. Meat, honey, and ale. We need to get his strength up.'

Janiver curtsied. 'My lord.' She followed the group back to Nathaniel's quarters.

***

Nathaniel missed Tad. His quick sense of humor. The repartee, the banter. Even the arguments. He missed talking to someone that knew what a motor vehicle was. Or an airplane. Movies, television. An ice machine. A foreman grill. Heated toilet seats. Okay—the Marine knew that none of that existed anymore. But it used to, or it would. Whatever, the fact that you could talk about it was enough.

Here, in amongst the clans, it was all, "my lord this and my lord that". Lord Nathaniel, Lord Degeo, Lord Arnthor, The Forever Man. So many names. He missed being Sergeant Hogan. Life was simpler then.

And, once again, Nathaniel wondered if any of this was real. Was he an almost immortal, time-traveling superhero with a geas to unite the tribes and save the Picts from Roman subjugation? And then would he somehow be transported back to his own time? Did he then have to continue his geas?

Or, was he simply a complete loon and, even now, was lying in some hospital bed in London? Drugged to the eyeballs and under full-time supervision as he had suffered the mother of all breaks from reality and had become a fully certified basket case?

He poked at the fire in front of him with a stick and watched the sparks fly up into the frigid morning sky. He sat in a camp amongst over two thousand other warriors. He was waiting.

After another half an hour the druid returned on horseback, dismounted and walked up to the Marine.

'My lord. Chief Cradoc has accepted your challenge. You will fight tonight. By firelight. However, my lord, he has demanded unarmed combat.'

Nathaniel shrugged. 'Whatever.'

The druid shook his head. 'I agreed with his demands, lord, as I knew that you would insist but, I must warn you. Cradoc has never been beaten before in unarmed trial.'

'Big bastard, is he?' enquired Nathaniel.

'Not so much big as,' the druid hesitated. 'Large.'

'What's the difference?'

'Well,' continued Torkill. 'If I said that he was fat, you would get the wrong impression. But I suppose that one could call him fat.'

Padan snorted. 'He's the size of a house,' he said. 'Maybe six foot tall but must weigh five hundred pounds plus. If he gets hold of you, my lord, you are a dead man. Trust me; I've seen him crush someone so badly that when he was finished there wasn't a single connected bone left in his entire body. Like a bag of mud, he was.'

'Well, I'll keep far away and jab him to death,' replied Nathaniel.

Padan and Torkill stared at each another. Eventually Padan spoke.

'You tell him.'

The druid took a deep breath. 'You can't keep away. You'll be tied together. Separated by a four-foot-long leather strap, tied to each of your left wrists.'

Nathaniel put his head in his hands. 'Damn it,' he said. 'Anything else?'

They both shook their heads.

'Okay then,' said the Marine. 'Let me rest. I know it's still morning, but I haven't had much sleep lately. If you need anything, ask Janiver. Wake me two hours before we set off.'

He stood up from the fire, went to his tent, crawled under his furs, and lay there. Thinking once again of double-shot espresso lattes and fudge brownies and computer games. As opposed to being tied to a five-hundred-pound gorilla and fighting to the death.

Needless to say—sleep took a while to come.

CHAPTER 9

Janiver brushed the hair back from Padraig's face and wiped the sweat from him with a damp, cool cloth. The young man was healing well, his wounds had been stitched and there was no mortification present. Also, he was young and fit, so he had every chance of recovering.

As he lay sleeping he looked younger than his nineteen years, his face unlined apart from the lines of pain. His body was a physical poem. Long limbed, his muscles smooth and even, not yet having achieved the bulk and the coarseness of a fully-grown male warrior. The rows of stitches stood out like fissures in marble and his bruises as dark shadows on a landscape of virgin snow.

When he was awake his eyes were of

the deepest azure, his brows thick and noble and his default expression one of mild bafflement. As if the world and all of its evils both puzzled and saddened him.

He moaned in his sleep. Either nightmares or pain, Janiver could not be sure. So, she took his hand and held it tight, attempting to draw his pain from him. She sat with him all of that day and that night, willing him to heal.

The next morning, when he awoke, hers was the first face that he saw.

And he smiled.

She stroked his face.

***

Nathaniel had zero fight plan whatsoever. Massive bonfires had been lit all around the fighting circle and thousands of warriors had formed a vast ring around the area.

Opposite the Marine stood the largest man that he had ever seen. Not the tallest, in fact he was almost half a foot shy of Nathaniel's six feet five inches. But he was simply enormous.

Nathaniel remembered when he had once been stationed to Japan and had gone to watch a Sumo wrestling match. Afterwards he had been privileged enough to actually meet the Yokozuna, the top wrestler. It was like meeting a mountain, albeit a talking, breathing, sentient one. He remembered that the Yokozuna weighed about 480 pounds. And he had been a lightweight compared to the monstrous Pict standing opposite him. The man's arms were far bigger than Nathaniel's legs and his legs were like tree trunks. His belly hung down in massive pendulous folds almost to his knees and his chins blended into his chest like a waterfall of lard.

But the sheer weight was not the only thing that worried Nathaniel. The simple fact of the matter is that, anyone who spends every day carrying around a surplus weight of almost half a ton is going to be very, very strong.

Chief Cradoc's druid stepped forward

and bowed to Nathaniel. Then he took a four-foot length of leather from his robes and tied the one end securely around the Marine's left wrist. He led the Marine into the center of the circle and joined him to Chief Cradoc, tying off the other end to the fat man's left wrist. Then he stood back.

'Warriors,' he said. 'Fight.'

Nathaniel reacted immediately, bringing his right knee up and then unleashing a massive roundhouse kick to Cradoc's face. It was like trying to chop down a mountain with a hammer. The fat man flinched but did not move.

Nathaniel did it again. This time he was rewarded by the sight of blood as the skin over the fat man's left eye split.

Nathaniel stepped in closer and launched a massive straight right into the same eye. He struck Cradoc's face so hard that he felt the shock through his whole body. The cut opened up and blood streamed down Cradoc's face.

Emboldened by his success, Nathaniel lifted his knee to his chest and slammed his heel into Cradoc's enormous gut. It was a complete waste of time, so he went back to punching him in the face.

Nathaniel struck again and again until his fist was bruised and painful and the fat man's face was covered in blood.

The Marine tried for another kick to the head. But this time, as he unleashed the kick, Cradoc moved with surprising speed, grabbed his foot and lifted, throwing the Marine to the ground. Then the fat man lent forward, grabbed Nathaniel by his hair, lifted him with ease and enveloped him in a gigantic, stinking, sweaty bear hug.

'Got you now, wee man,' grunted Cradoc. 'Gave you a fair chance I did, but you wasted it. Now—time to die.'

Nathaniel felt his ribs begin to creak from the pressure of the bear hug. His right arm was still free, and he hammered it down on top of the fat man's skull, but to no avail.

He began to see black spots in front of his eyes as the lack of oxygen started to affect his vision. Then the world turned to gray.

He vividly remembered the taste of the Lagavulan single malt scotch that he had ordered once at the bar of the Connaught hotel in London. The smell of boot polish from his time training on Parris Island. His mother's voice. The sound of an M16 assault rifle firing on full auto. His sister's laughter.

Something broke inside him and the pain brought him, momentarily, back into the land of the living.

He stared around him. At the baying faces of the Pictish warriors. The concerned face of Torkill, his druid. And he thought of Janiver, his love and his destiny. He let his mind spread. He let his consciousness flow. Out. Out. Seeking, delving deep into the earth and high into the sky. And there he found it. Not in massive quantities like it was during his time of the pulse, but it was still there. The magic. The power. Gamma rays from the Aurora Borealis.

The silver weave of his mental net settled down over the swimming shreds of power and he reeled them in, pulling them close. Tight to him.

Firstly, he used them to strengthen his muscles, turning them to steel to resist Cradoc's crushing embrace. Then he healed himself, knitting his ribs, repairing his ruptured spleen, his punctured lung.

Finally, he powered the rest of it into his muscles.

He grabbed Cradoc's right wrist and simply pulled it away from him, breaking the bear hug in an instant. The look of utter surprise on the fat man's face was almost comical as the Marine placed his right hand on his bloated chest and shoved. Cradoc lifted off his feet and flew through the air like an extremely mobile hippo, snapping the leather connection as he did so and landing with an earth-shaking thump.

Nathaniel strode over to him and delivered a chopping right and left to his head. The fat man rolled to the floor, gasping as he tried to get his breath back. Eventually he stood up, legs shaky, air whistling in and out as his massive chest heaved like a blacksmith's bellows.

'It's over,' said Nathaniel. 'Swear fealty to me and you shall live. I shall even let you stay as leader of your own tribe. Simply swear your life to mine and that will be the end.'

Cradoc shook his head. 'I don't think so, wee man. A couple of lucky shots does not a victor make.' He shambled forward, arms outstretched as he attempted to ensnare the Marine once again.

Nathaniel danced inside the fat man's arms and struck him with a cracking right cross, followed by a left hook and another straight right. Blood sprayed from Cradoc's face and forehead as the blows carved into him.

'Submit,' shouted Nathaniel. 'Swear fealty. Don't be stupid.'

'Up yours, little man,' bellowed Cradoc in return. 'It's your time to die.' He rushed forward again, moving surprisingly quickly on his massive tree-trunk legs.

It was with a certain amount of regret that Nathaniel delivered his final blow. He went down on one knee and delivered a straight-armed punch to the center of Cradoc's meaty chest as the huge man charged down on him. The Marine's fist sank almost to his elbow into the fat and flesh of the big man. Nathaniel could hear ribs breaking. He could feel flesh tearing. Blood squirted out of Cradoc's nose and eyes and, with a look of absolute incredulity on his face, the big man keeled over.

Dead.

The crowd of warriors went wild.

CHAPTER 10

Nathaniel now controlled nine of the twenty clans of the Picts. The last one he had gained without ritual combat. Chief Feargus had arrived some two weeks ago and sworn fealty without battle. He was happy to call Nathaniel his king as long as he still maintained nominal leadership of his own tribe.

Padraig sat opposite him, tearing the flesh off a leg of mutton and eating with great relish. It was now six weeks in all since the young man had arrived and he was almost fully recovered.

Nathaniel found him to be sharp of wit and deep thinking. He was an honorable man and, after the Marine had sparred with him in training, he saw that he was also a fine warrior. He was particularly gifted with the light javelin or throwing lance and could even hit a target whilst throwing from the back of a galloping horse, a task that few others could emulate.

Nathaniel had immediately gotten Padraig to teach the cavalry how to handle a throwing lance in the same fashion, and he had officially named Padraig as his lancelord in charge of the cavalry.

Since Nathaniel had managed to use The Power in his fight with Cradoc, Torkill the druid had spent many hours with him, training, teaching control, getting him to meditate and showing him exercises so that he could get into the same mental space that he was in when he had fought the fat man.

But it was no use. Nathaniel could sense the power. He could almost feel it. But he couldn't control it. It slipped away from him, touching the outer reaches of his consciousness, flirting with his subconscious but never showing itself in full. The frustration was driving the Marine mental.

Janiver came up behind him and

started to massage his shoulders in an attempt to ease the tension out of him. After a few minutes Nathaniel stood up, brushing her hands from him.

'I have to see Padan,' he said. 'He needs to set up a challenge with Chief MacAsgain. I need more of the clans to follow me before I can rule.'

The Marine swept from the room in search of his right-hand man and his druid, ignoring Janiver completely.

The queen-in-waiting stood where she was, hands by her side, a slight glaze of tears in her eyes.

'He means no harm, my lady,' said Padraig, sensing Janiver's confusion and distress at her lord's sharp behavior. 'He is under enormous stress. He has to lead the clans, he has naught to look forward to but yet another in a line of mortal combats and, even then, who knows whether the present king will accede or declare war?'

Janiver wiped a tear. 'He has changed, Padraig.'

'Aye, mistress. He has. But then, who

wouldn't?'

'He is not like us, Padraig. He is different.'

The young warrior nodded. 'Truth you speak, lady. I suspect that our Lord Arnthor Degeo may be a god.'

Janiver nodded. 'I too think thus,' she agreed. 'So, tell me, Padraig, do you think that gods are capable of true love?'

The young man shrugged. 'They are capable of what they are capable of, my lady. It is not ours to question.'

'And you, Padraig?' asked Janiver. 'Are you capable of love or is your heart too full of hate for the Romans to allow such a trivial emotion to intercede?'

Padraig stared at the queen-in-waiting, his dark eyes bored into her. 'I am capable of love, lady. For love is not a trivial thing, it is the most powerful of all emotions.'

'So. Whom do you love then, young warrior chief?'

'I love my people,' said Padraig. 'I love my lord Nathaniel Arnthor Degeo and

I love you, mistress.'

Janiver blushed but hid it by turning her head away from the intense young man.

'You love me?' She smiled.

'With all my heart,' assured Padraig. 'For are you not a living part of my lord Degeo? And, as such, I shall love you as much as I love him.'

And because Janiver was facing away from him, the young man could not see the look of disappointment on her face. Nor would he have understood it even if he had seen it.

'Is there anything that I can do for you, lady?' he asked. 'For, if not then I need to continue my training of the cavalry.'

Janiver waved him away without looking up or speaking.

Padraig left the tent, collecting his batch of lances as he did so.

CHAPTER 11

True to his word, when Padraig had fully recovered he took one hundred men with him and went on a field trip to visit his relatives.

Firstly, he visited his brother in law, Chief Dunbar. Secondly, his uncle, Chief MacVaxtar and, finally, his godfather, Chief Gillanders.

All three of them agreed to join under the banner of Lord Nathaniel Arnthor Degeo.

Padraig gave them two weeks to get their troops in order and then, he informed them, the banner of Degeo would march on the king.

Nathaniel now controlled thirteen of the twenty Pictish clans.

The next two weeks were frantic as

Nathaniel and his chiefs drew together to form one of the greatest armies that the Picts had ever seen.

They formed up on the plains of Kilbride and marched, twenty thousand strong, to the castle of King Tavish MacDonell of clan Ranald in Dunblane.

And their arrival was as a host from the gods so mighty was their presence.

However, it had taken them over two weeks to march there, so King MacDonell had been offered ample time to bring up his own clans. And he had done so.

Fully fifteen thousand men.

For the first time since Nathaniel had met him, Torkill the druid looked nervous.

'This is simply a war waiting to happen, my lord,' he informed Nathaniel.

'Not on my watch,' retorted the Marine. 'Send messengers out to all of our men. I am going in alone, tell them to stay put. That means without you, or Padan or Padraig. Just me, under a banner of truce.'

Torkill shook his head. 'I don't

recommend that. Lord, please, at least take Padan and me with you.'

'Can the two of you fight fifteen thousand men?'

Torkill shook his head.

'Well then,' continued Nathaniel. 'What's the point?

No, druid, I go alone.'

The Marine waited until the message had been sent to his men. Meanwhile, Padraig had taken a lance and attached a white banner to it. He handed it to Nathaniel.

'Take care, my lord,' he said.

Nathaniel winked at him. 'Always, my friend. Always.'

The Marine nudged his horse in the flanks, trotting forward towards King MacDonell's host, the banner of truce billowing in the wind as he held it high.

It took Nathaniel about twenty minutes to cross the space between the two armies and, when he was still a few hundred paces out, he noticed a single horseman riding towards him. As he approached closer, the Marine could see that it was none other than King Tavish MacDonell himself. Riding alone.

The king drew up in front of the Marine and nodded his greeting.

'Well met, Lord Nathaniel Arnthor Degeo.'

'Aye,' agreed Nathaniel. 'Well met, King Tavish MacDonell of clan Ranald.'

'So, young man,' continued the king. 'Do you come to my lands in an effort to do war upon me?'

Nathaniel shook his head. 'Nay, sire. However, I do come to challenge you for the seat of the throne of the Picts.'

'And if you win?'

'When I win,' corrected the Marine. 'When I win, I shall unite the Pictish tribes against the Romans and push them back from our lands. I shall punish them so that they never strike against us again, such will be their fear of the Pictish people.'

The king shook his head. 'Dreams of

mist and sand, young man. The Romans cannot be beaten. I myself have warred against them. I have attacked them with overwhelming odds in our advantage and they have decimated us at every turn. Even your friend Padraig and his two thousand warriors were annihilated by less than five hundred Romans and it is said, that they lost but three men in return. Also, we Picts are not full-time warriors.'

The king waved his hand to encompass the host of men around him.

'One looks and sees thirty-five thousand men in battle gear. But I see thirty-five thousand farmers carrying swords. Aye, there is none braver, none more stalwart nor courageous in battle than these men who stand around us but, the fact is, they are homemakers first and warriors second. I do not know where you have come from, Lord Degeo, and I have no doubt that you are a fearsome warrior, but you must understand, when these men go to war you will be lucky to take twenty thousand with you. The others will have to stay behind to protect their livestock and families from wolves and bears. They will need to plant and to till. They will have to continue the tasks that keep us all alive through the lean winter months.'

'I hear what you say, King MacDonell,' agreed Nathaniel. 'But I feel that we may not have a choice. I do not think that the latest punitive action by the Romans was their last. They have become emboldened with their easy wins and, it will not be long before they begin to encroach on our home soil.'

'There are twenty thousand Romans on the wall itself,' said King MacDonell. 'It is rumored that the Ninth legion is encamped close by and, if we create too much of a stir, then the emperor could send a force as large as forty thousand against us. They would annihilate us. It would be the end of my people.'

'No,' Nathaniel disagreed. 'It would be the end of Roman dominance. Under my leadership we would destroy any attempt by the emperor to subjugate us. Trust me, we can, and we will, successfully engage the Romans. They are not superhuman. They are not even fighting for their own lands and their own people. They are mere mercenaries. We can take them.'

King MacDonell looked deeply into the young warrior's eyes and saw absolute belief. And more, he saw wisdom. An understanding that far superseded mere age. In fact, when he looked into Nathaniel's eyes he saw an infinity of knowledge. Comprehension and understanding without end. He saw—The Forever Man.

And the king climbed off his horse and knelt in front of The Forever Man. He drew his sword and laid it on the ground.

Nathaniel dismounted and stood opposite the kneeling king.

'I swear fealty, my Lord Nathaniel Arnthor Degeo,' said the king. 'My sword, my life, my people and my kingdom are yours to command. The fate of the Pictish nation is now held in your palm.' He looked up at Nathaniel. 'A nation lives or dies at your will, Lord Degeo. Take stock of that thought and remember it well in these coming days.'

Nathaniel drew his axe and held it out to the ex-king who lent forward and kissed the blade. 'My life,' the ex-king said.

'And my honor,' answered Nathaniel.

The Marine grasped MacDonell by the hand and helped him to his feet.

And the sound of over thirty thousand cheering warriors thundered across the valley, shaking the ground, and raising the birds to flight as, for the first time, the Pictish clans were fully united.

CHAPTER 12

In the castle of MacDonell stood a massive, ancient, round table that could seat upwards of thirty people. At the moment Nathaniel, Torkill the druid, Padan, Padraig, and the twenty clan chiefs sat around it. A fire blazed in the huge hearth, managing to heat half of the room but leaving the other half frigid and slightly damp. MacDonell sat on Nathaniel's right-hand side and the rest of the Marine's entourage sat on his left.

Nathaniel stood up.

'Lords,' he said. 'Today is the culmination of many months of fighting and bleeding and killing. Today is the day that I have been striving for, at the possible cost of my own life. Today is the first day in the beginning of the end of the Roman's encroachment on our land. But, before we discuss details I want to ask of you all one question. Why do the Romans win all of their battles? They seldom have superior numbers, they are no braver than us and their equipment, although different, is not inherently superior. Yet they win. Always. Why?'

'Discipline,' said one of the chiefs.

'Are we not disciplined?' asked Nathaniel. 'Are they so much more disciplined than us?'

The chief shook his head. 'Tactics,' said another.

'We too have tactics,' replied the Marine. 'Are our tacticians so much worse than theirs?'

Again, a shaking of heads in denial.

Nathaniel picked up a Roman gladius short sword that had been lying on the table in front of him. He held it high.

'This,' he said. 'This is why the Romans win.' Then, using his fingers he spanned the tip of the gladius and some three inches of blade. 'These first three inches of the Roman gladius. Because the Romans have learned that three inches of sharpened steel is enough to kill a man. Whereas we insist on using six feet of broadsword. Because of that, we need space in which to fight. One on one, the Pict is the most fearsome warrior the world has ever known. But in formation we are simply a group of brave individuals. The Romans are a machine that exists only to plunge those three inches of steel into the enemy's body. Every formation, every tactic that they have, centers on that one simple fact. And therein lies their weakness.'

Nathaniel left his seat and walked around the table, gladius held out in front of him.

'The tortoise, the wedge, the saw. All of these formations allow the Roman soldier to protect himself from attack whilst, at the same time, they allow him to part his shield wall just enough to poke this crappy little sword out and stab us.'

The Marine slammed the sword into the table where it vibrated with the shock.

'Well, no more,' he shouted. 'From this day on I will show you how to take this advantage away from the Romans and turn it into his greatest disadvantage. Over the next few weeks I will teach you and then you will go home and teach your men. Within the following three months we will become the very stuff of nightmares for the Romans. We will become their nadir and their bane. For eons to come, people will talk about us in hushed sentences as they recall what we did to the mighty Roman Empire. Through us, the name of the Picts shall live forever.'

There was a tumultuous cheering as the chiefs sprang to their feet as one, and bellowed Nathaniel's name.

'Degeo, Degeo, Degeo!'

***

The next few weeks were the busiest of Nathaniel's life. Firstly, he had to change hundreds of years of traditional Pictish battle tactics that consisted mainly of lining up in front of the enemy and charging into them, six-foot broadsword windmilling about and chopping up all and any who came close enough.

Secondly, he set out to radically increase the size of the Pictish cavalry. He did this by commandeering every horse of the correct size in the kingdom and then setting every saddlemaker and leathersmith in the area to make saddles and tack.

He then commanded all blacksmiths to mass-produce light lances for throwing. Thousands upon thousands of them. Nathaniel aimed to have a cavalry of lancers at least fifteen thousand strong. Almost half of his entire force. He did this because he knew, from his history lessons that he had learned over a thousand years into the future, that the Romans were at their weakest against cavalry. Especially mounted archers.

He didn't have enough time to train mounted archers, but he could train lance throwers, particularly with the help of Lancelord Padraig.

Then lay the task of explaining the concept of guerilla warfare. Or what the clan chiefs had termed "run away fighting". He was busy at the moment trying, once again, to put the seemingly simple concept across.

'So,' said Padan. 'You're saying that we attack the Romans, chuck a few lances at them, inflict a couple of casualties and then run away?'

Nathaniel nodded. 'Basically, yes. Then we wait until they've all relaxed and we do it again. Sometimes we dig trench traps for them to fall into or we simply set fire to the food wagon.'

'And then run away again,' confirmed Padan.

'Yep.'

The red-bearded warrior shook his head. Nathaniel noticed that many of the other warrior chiefs were reacting the same way.

'Can't see how a battle can be won by constantly running away,' said Padan.

'It can't,' agreed Nathaniel. 'But by using those tactics one can, eventually, win a war. Constant striking at an enemy by a smaller force keeps them from relaxing. They have to constantly be on guard. Their supply lines are disrupted. One can draw them deeper into enemy territory and cause them to be cut off. And then, when they are in the perfect place for us to strike hard—we do so. With overwhelming force.'

'Okay, lord,' said MacDonell. 'We shall take your word for it. Now, what about all of this cavalry? It has never been our tradition to fight on horseback. Two feet on the ground and a good sword is our way.'

'The Romans have a weakness against cavalry,' answered Nathaniel. 'Their formations are deadly but slow to move. Even when they run, it is more shuffle than sprint. Lancer cavalry can strike and withdraw. Injuring without taking losses. And the Romans have little cavalry, so they will have no answer.'

MacDonell nodded, albeit reluctantly.

'There is one more request that I need to make of you,' continued Nathaniel. He held up a spiked object made up of two short lengths of spiked steel bent and welded together in the middle. When he threw it onto the table one could see that, however it landed, one sharpened spike would always be sticking up. 'This is a caltrop. You scatter them on the ground so that, when the Romans march forward, it penetrates the leather soles of their sandals and seriously ruins their day.'

This small witticism was greeted by a round of laughter.

'This simple piece of steel will be guaranteed to break up any Roman advance and, as we know, a splintered Roman advance is to our advantage. One on one, we can defeat them. As a coherent unit, we cannot. I will give each of you a handful of these and I ask that you get your blacksmiths to make as many as they can over the next few weeks. We need hundreds of thousands of them. Enough to booby-trap an entire battlefield.'

There was a murmuring of assent

amongst the clan chiefs.

'Right then,' said Nathaniel as he stood up again. 'Go. Do it. Train your men in the arts that Padraig has shown you, manufacture the caltrops. Return as soon as you can.'

The clan chiefs stood and saluted as one, then they filed from the room.

Padraig, the druid, and Padan followed them, leaving The Forever Man alone.

After a while Janiver came in. As always, she was dressed in flowing white, her hair controlled by a circlet of gold. Around her neck a torc of ebony that set off her milky white, flawless skin.

She walked over and sat on Nathaniel's lap.

'You are tense, my lord,' she said. 'It grows late. Come to bed and I will help you to relax.' She nuzzled into his neck, her tongue flicked at his chin and lips. Pink. Small. Like a cat.

Nathaniel kissed her passionately. 'I cannot, my sweet,' he answered. 'Chief

Gillanders did not show today. He sent message that he was ill but there are rumors that he is having second thoughts. If he pulls out, then many other clans might follow. He is a man with influence, particularly with the highland tribes. I need to leave tonight. I will travel by torchlight, rest after midnight and get there first thing in the morning.'

'Send Padan and Torkill,' argued Janiver.

'Alas, I cannot,' said Nathaniel. 'I lead, so I must go.' He took her hand and kissed the palm. 'This pace will not continue forever, my love. Soon I will have more time for you.'

The Marine picked her off his lap and stood up, kissing her once more before he left the room, calling for Padan and Torkill as he did so.

Janiver waited until he had left and then she picked up a water goblet from the table and threw it against the wall, screaming out her frustration.

Janiver stood on the battlements and watched the torchlight from Nathaniel's party fade into the night as they rode away.

Then she turned and walked back into the depths of the castle. Although the castle was large and the corridors many and meandering she knew where she was going and walked with sure foot and obvious knowledge. After a few minutes she came to a door and, without knocking, she opened it and walked in.

Padraig sat on the edge of his bed. He wore only a loincloth and a band of leather around his head to keep his hair out of his eyes. At his feet lay a pile of throwing lances. In his hand he held another lance. He was sharpening the tip with a wet stone, methodically working it along the edges of the spear so that they glowed red in the light from the fire. Such was his concentration that he didn't, at first, notice that Janiver had entered the room. It was only when she cleared her throat that he looked up.

'My queen.'

Janiver laughed. The sound as light as silver thread. 'Not yet, Padraig,' she said. 'Lord Arnthor and I are not yet married.'

'A mere formality, my queen,' insisted the lancelord. He stood up and walked across the room to fetch a tunic to cover himself. But before he reached his wardrobe Janiver stopped him with a hand on his arm.

'There is no need to enrobe on my behalf, Padraig,' she whispered. 'After all, I have seen you naked before when I was nursing you back to health.'

The young warrior shook his head.

'It is unseemly, lady,' he said as he gently pulled away from her. He grabbed a doeskin tunic and dragged it over his head.

Janiver laughed again. But this time her laughter was less light. Throatier. Salacious.

Padraig blushed a deep red and looked away from her.

She walked over to his bed and sat down on it. Patted the mattress next to her.

Padraig snatched at his kilt and hastily buckled it on. 'I must apologize, my queen,' he muttered. 'I have things to do.'

He bowed and swiftly left the room.

Behind him he heard Janiver's laughter once again. Low and husky and dangerous.

Full of promise.

Of fruits forbidden.

CHAPTER 13

Although Nathaniel had planned on taking a break sometime after midnight he changed his mind and the three of them, himself, Padan, and Torkill, pushed on through the night.

They arrived at Chief Gillanders' settlement at around two hours before sunrise. Nathaniel was surprised to see that the main gates were open, and no sentry had been set.

'Now here is a man who is not afraid of the Romans,' said Padan.

'Nor brigands,' added Torkill.

'Look to your weapons,' said Nathaniel. 'I like this not. Look,' he pointed towards Gillanders' sprawling abode. In front of it was a lavishly appointed, two-wheeled Roman carpentum. A covered wagon used by the Roman senatorial class or anyone of wealth and influence. The horses had been detached and were obviously in the stables. Again, there were neither guards nor sentries.

The abode itself was silent and dark. The household still asleep. Even the servants would not start to rise until at least one hour before sunrise when bread would be baked, and breakfast prepared.

The three men dismounted and tethered their horses to the hitching post outside the main door. They drew their weapons. Nathaniel his axe, Padan his broadsword, and Torkill his vicious, razor-sharp sickle.

The front door was latched but it was a simple exercise for Padan to insert his broadsword through the gap in the side of the door and lift the bar. The hinges were well greased with animal fat and the door swung open silently.

The three warriors padded down the passageway towards the sleeping area of the huge house. Torkill, who had been a guest of Gillanders' before, led the way.

'There,' he whispered and pointed. Lying, curled up on the floor in front of a door, was a young man dressed in a short Roman tunic. Obviously, a servant of some sort, sleeping outside his master's room so as to be at his constant beck and call.

'Romans,' grunted Padan.

'And sleeping in the room reserved for honored guests,' added Torkill.

'Come on,' whispered Nathaniel. 'Let's take a look at this Roman.'

The three of them sneaked towards the door but, as quiet as they were, the servant awoke and jumped to his feet. But, before he could utter a sound, Torkill's scythe struck him in the throat, severing his vocal cords and his arteries in one fell swoop. Blood jetted high and the servant fell, twitching, to the ground.

Nathaniel raised an eyebrow. 'Bit harsh.'

Torkill shrugged. 'He would have

raised the alarm.'

The Marine eased the door handle down and pushed the door open. The room inside was large and sumptuously furnished. Hand woven carpets, carved wooden seats, and a small table. The windows were shuttered but the fire was still glowing in the hearth, providing ample light for which to see.

A naked, corpulent man of advancing middle age lay snoring on the bed, his massive gut rising and falling to the sound of his porcine breathing.

Nathaniel walked over and prodded him in the stomach with the blade of his axe.

'Hey, Roman,' he said. 'Rise and shine.'

The foreigner spluttered awake, rubbing his eyes as he did so.

'What is the meaning of this?' he demanded.

'What you doing here?' asked Nathaniel.

'I am a guest,' blurted the Roman. 'And an important one at that, so, peasant, I advise you to leave my room this instant or things will go very badly for you.'

'I'm not a peasant,' said Nathaniel. 'I'm a Marine. Oorah!'

'What?' asked the Roman, his eyes wide with incredulity at Nathaniel's audacity.

The Marine shook his head. 'Whatever.'

He swung the axe in a tight circle, striking the Roman's neck just below his Adam's apple and causing it to leap from his torso like a scalded cat.

Nathaniel grabbed the dismembered head by its short hair and picked it up.

'Come on,' he said to his companions. 'Let's go have a chat to Chief Gillanders and ask him about our Roman friend here.'

They filed from the room and let themselves into Gillanders' room that was situated at the end of the corridor.

Nathaniel stood over the sleeping

body of the chief and then, with a mighty swipe, he smashed him in the face with the severed Roman head.

'Wake up, you cowardly traitor,' he shouted.

Gillanders came instantly awake, jackknifing into a sitting position, his arms and legs jerking spasmodically as he did so.

'What the …'

Before he finished his sentence, Nathaniel hit him in the face with the head again. Then The Forever Man grasped Gillanders by his ear and pulled his face close to the Roman head, their noses almost touching. 'What the hell is this Roman doing in my kingdom?' he shouted.

Gillanders screamed in terror, still half asleep, covered in blood, his vision full of severed head.

Nathaniel threw the bloody head into the corner and dragged Gillanders from his bed, holding him up by the front of his tunic.

'Talk, Gillanders. What's happening?'

'It's not what you think, my lord.'

'How do you know?' snapped Nathaniel. 'How do you know what I'm thinking?'

'It's just that, my lord, the Romans … I was …'

'I know what you were doing, Gillanders,' said Nathaniel. 'You were making a deal with the Romans. You were selling out to our enemy. The enemy of our people. Why? For gods sakes, why?'

The chief stared at Nathaniel for a while and then he seemed to regain his senses. And a semblance of his pride. He stood straighter and brushed the Marine's grip from his tunic.

'Because in your way lies madness,' he said. 'Your way is suicide. The suicide of a nation. Of an entire people. You cannot beat the Romans. It's impossible. Your inflated ego will be the death of our people.'

'So, you did a deal with the devil,'

answered Nathaniel. 'What did you promise?'

Gillanders took a deep breath and then looked away.

'Talk, Gillanders,' prompted the Marine. 'Tell me or I shall let the druid question you.'

The chief went pale as the blood drained from his face. 'No, my lord. Have mercy.'

'Then talk.'

'I promised your head, lord. Delivered to the Romans on a plate.'

Nathaniel laughed. 'Ironic, isn't it?'

'What, my lord?' asked Gillanders.

'That, instead of my head on a plate they shall be getting their envoy's head in a bag.' The Marine laughed again, but the sound was devoid of humor.

Chief Gillanders allowed himself a small, sick-looking smile.

'Oh,' continued Nathaniel. 'And, of course, they also get a bonus head. Yours.'

The axe sang. Gillanders' head tumbled to the floor and his body followed, slumping silently to its knees, and then pitching forward in a gout of blood.

'The Roman envoy will have come with guards,' said Nathaniel to Padan. 'Find them. Give them the two heads and a message. Tell them, there will be blood for blood. Tell them that The Forever Man waits for them. Druid, come with me. We need to wake Gillanders' private guards and explain things to them. If they're lucky, then I won't kill them. But first, I need to know who else is involved in this scheme.'

Torkill led Nathaniel from the room while Padan wrapped the two severed heads in a blanket and threw them over his shoulder to make carrying easier.

CHAPTER 14

Nathaniel observed the Romans from afar, using the trees as cover. Emperor Severus had taken a dim view of Nathaniel's presentation of the head of the Roman envoy. He had been even more insulted by Nathaniel's threats.

It had taken him a while but, finally, he had sent his vaunted Ninth legion far beyond Hadrian's Wall to administer chastisement. He had told them to find the nearest large settlement of Picts and destroy them utterly. Then they were to sow the land with salt and burn every forest that they came upon. The Picts were to remember the might of the Roman Empire for years to come.

However, Nathaniel had preempted this strike and he had commanded the evacuation and withdrawal of all Picts within a hundred miles of the wall. As a result, the Romans had to march much deeper into enemy territory than they would normally have considered prudent.

The Ninth legion stood six thousand strong and, even at distance, the Marine could see that these were tough men. Men who had fought, unbeaten, across Hispania, hence their nickname, the Hispanica legion.

Carrying sword and shield and finely pointed javelin, along with full kit, weighing perhaps forty or fifty pounds per man, the legion marched all day at the steady military pace of twenty miles in five hours. Every night, march complete, they would then set down their kit and build a full camp, including ditches and palisades and gateways, in exactly the same plan as any legionary fortress.

Then, every morning at around the same time, about an hour before sunrise, they would awaken, eat breakfast, and form up to march again.

It was at this time that they were at

their most vulnerable. For it was in the early morning that the highland mists shrouded all in an impenetrable whiteout. And in the mist, was death.

Under the cover of the mist, the Picts would sneak in and kill as many as they could. Swiftly and silently. Then they would behead them and bring the heads back to their camp. Later in the day these heads would be discovered by the Romans on top of stakes hammered into the ground.

The losses were not many. Ten, maybe fifteen legionnaires a day. Not enough to warrant staying in the camp until midmorning every day. But still enough to affect morale.

As well as this, the legion was now starting to run out of supplies, apart from the ubiquitous barley that was universally hated by the Roman soldiers and was referred to as animal feed. But there was no way that they could supplement their diet with either game nor wheat as Nathaniel's men had cleared the land of all and any sustenance, from edible roots to the smallest of game.

Now, after two full weeks, the Ninth was into the hills and mountains of the Highlands.

This was Nathaniel's chosen killing ground. It was here that he had decided to end, forever, the myth of Roman invincibility. And he aimed to do this by destroying the venerated Ninth legion. Emperor Severus' favorite legion and the most feared and successful of all of the Roman fighting units.

The foothills of the Highland mountains formed many folds and vales in the land. Coarse heather and piles of scree made footing all the more treacherous and, for Nathaniel and his warriors, this was a perfect area for an ambush.

The Romans had just forged the Derry Burn River and were marching into the Cairngorms, their marching order strung out as they were forced into the narrow valleys and folds of the foothills.

Nathaniel had led the Romans into this specific valley by allowing them to catch glimpses of his warriors running before them as well as releasing small deer that he had captured so that attention was drawn forward into the twisting valley. The Romans were so confident of their military superiority that they had the bare minimum of scouts in front of the main column. However, even if they had scouted in force it would have done them little good. Nathaniel's men were Highland born. To them the heather and gorse was their birthright and they could conceal themselves better than the wild animals that roved the hills.

The column of six-thousand legionnaires marched five abreast and stretched back for almost a mile. Along the hills on each side of the valley, Nathaniel had placed ten thousand of his warriors, five thousand on each side. Aside from their usual broadsword and shield, he had equipped each of these warriors with a sling and a pouch full of lead shot. Every Pict had used the sling since early childhood and they were capable of bringing down small game such as hare or even deer at almost four hundred yards.

He had also issued them with a bundle of five light javelins as well as one long, twelve-foot, broad-bladed heavy spear. Across a pinch in the valley he had dug deep trenches with sharpened spikes at the base. He had then covered them with a latticework of light branches and grass so as to conceal them from all but the minutest scrutiny.

Finally, around the back of one of the small hills, he had two thousand cavalry. Five hundred of these riders each carried a large leather bag of steel caltrops. Perhaps one hundred thousand of them all told.

They waited.

As the first row of the Roman column reached the trenches the leading legionnaires fell in and caused the entire column to stop. The rest of the column bunched up and lost their footing, cursing and shouting as the command to halt rippled down the line.

Nathaniel raised his hand and the horn blower next to him blew two long notes.

Immediately, the caltrop-carrying cavalry galloped around the hill and into the valley behind the Ninth legion. They galloped up as close as they could to the back of the column and then turned and bolted back, scattering the caltrops liberally as they did so.

The Ninth was now trapped between the spike-laden pits and the caltrop-strewn ground.

The horn blew again, and the Picts rose as one and started to unleash their lead missiles, working quickly until they were all expended. Hundreds of Romans lay wounded on the ground, heads, arms, and legs shattered by the vast quantities of lead shot that had rained down on them.

The horn bayed again and the Pictish warriors jogged down the hill towards the column.

But the Roman discipline was incredible as the legionnaires formed up again, locking together to form two shield walls, one facing each side of the valley.

When the Picts were a mere sixty yards away the horn blew again.

The warriors stopped and threw their javelins. One, two, three, four, five. A veritable storm of sharpened steel and wood fell on the Roman shield wall.

The horn bayed for the final time and the Highlanders picked up their heavy spears and charged, ululating and screaming as they came, ten thousand strong.

At the same time, the cavalry were charging as close as they could without reaching the caltrops, unleashing their throwing lances, launching them high into the air to come plunging down on the Roman soldiers.

On the other side of the trenches another thousand warriors unleashed their slingshots, raining lead down on the legionnaires.

The ten thousand Picts struck the Roman shield wall with a sound like thunder as the heavy spears slammed through shield and armor alike.

The Roman shield wall collapsed and, instead of a disciplined Roman formation there was now a group of individual soldiers with short swords, facing a superior number of the most deadly hand-to-hand combatants in the known world. The Highland warrior with a broadsword.

The slaughter continued late into the evening. Not one Roman survived. The cavalry cut down the last legionnaire by torchlight, some two miles away from the original battle.

The Ninth legion, the pride of Rome, was no more—and their standard now flew above Nathaniel Arnthor Degeo Hogan—The Forever Man.

CHAPTER 15

The clan chiefs were gathered about the huge round table in the keep of castle MacDonell. Vast quantities of uisge spirits, mead, and ale flowed like water. Servants carried platters of roast meats, vegetables, and bread.

In a dark corner of the room sat a pair of harpists, playing and singing heroic odes.

Padan stood up from the table and threw a half-eaten leg of mutton at the harpists.

'Shut it,' he shouted. 'Bloody fairy music. Play some bleeding pipes.'

The other chiefs joined in, banging their flagons on the table and throwing food at the harpists.

One of the musicians stood up, turned

his back on the chiefs and pulled up his kilt, flashed his hairy ass at them and farted loudly.

'There's some ass music for you, you red-bearded git,' he replied.

There was a round of good-natured laughter.

'By the gods,' shouted Padan. 'That's gruesome and all.'

The two musicians laid down their harps. One picked up a bag and pipes and started to prime them, blowing air into the bag. The other musician took out a bohdran frame drum and started to hammer out a savage beat. Rolling and thumping. A primal cadence that mimicked a speeding heartbeat.

Then the pipes started to lament. The spirit of the highlands issued forth, a low drone counter-pointed by the flute-like pipe chorus. It lilted and waxed and waned, changing from dirge to celebration, from poem to prose. Joy to woe.

And, in the valley around the castle, over forty thousand Highland men, women, and children celebrated the destruction of the Ninth and the prowess of their new king, The Forever Man.

***

Janiver lay naked on the bed and stared at Nathaniel. The firelight bathed her body in a warm, elemental glow that matched her inner ardor.

The Marine sat at a desk. In front of him were sheets of fine vellum and he was writing a list of commands and queries. Structures and plans, because he knew that the destruction of the Ninth would not go unpunished. And, unless he did something soon, the full might of Rome would fall upon the Picts and then, Forever Man or not, there was no way that the Picts could survive an assault from over a hundred thousand legionnaires.

'Come to bed, my lord.' Nathaniel shook his head.

'Soon, my sweet,' he said. 'I have to

plan our next steps. The following weeks will be crucial to our survival. Rest. I won't be long.'

The Marine worked hard, writing, consulting maps and sketching out battle plans. Eventually the candle started to gutter in its holder and he stopped.

But when he got to the bed it was empty.

Janiver had dressed and left and he had not even noticed.

He felt guilty and he promised himself that, as soon as he had solved the Roman problem, he would put aside time for her.

After all, she was to be his queen.

CHAPTER 16

Padraig ran hard. Wearing only his kilt and a pair of sandals and carrying his throwing lance he sprinted through the heather. Up hill and down dale. Every now and then he would halt, pick a distant target, such as a mound of gorse or a tree stump, throw the lance at it and then sprint to recover it.

He had been doing this since early morning. Punishing his body. Training far beyond what even the most rabid of perfectionists would consider enough. He had thrown up twice already and his breath was a constant burning in his lungs.

But still he pushed harder.

Eventually he came across a small stream and he threw himself into the frigid mountain water, gulping it down and splashing it over his overheated body. His stomach immediately went into a cramp as the cold water caused a vicious stitch. But he welcomed it. He welcomed the pain. The punishment. The self-chastisement.

Nathaniel Arnthor Degeo Hogan was his lord. And more. He was the leader of his people. He had taken him in when he was close to death. He had raised him to the position of lancelord and sat him at his right hand.

And in return Padraig had betrayed him. Utterly and completely.

She had come to him late last night. As she had many times before. And, as he had many times before, he had resisted. He had turned her away.

But his need for her was a physical pain. His desire a primal urge that he could not deny. Every waking moment was filled with visions of her face, her smell, her voice.

Which meant that, every waking moment was another moment spent betraying his lord.

He threw his head back and screamed

in anger and frustration.

And shame.

Then he ran back to the castle. He had made a decision. He knew that more battles were coming and, in the next one, he would put himself in the very vanguard of the fight. He would wear no armor, merely his kilt and sandals. If the gods spared him then he would consider his next punishment. If the gods decided to take his life, then he would accept their decision with open arms.

He felt better for his decision but continued to run as hard as he could. Still punishing himself.

***

Nathaniel knew that they had to strike now. Sooner rather than later.

Emperor Severus had started to mass troops in and around the fort of Sehedunum and already the 2nd, 6th and 20th legions were in base and battle ready.

Almost twenty thousand crack Roman legionnaires. If any more arrived, then Nathaniel doubted his ability to defeat them. Even twenty thousand was touch and go. For if he put every man that he could into the field, he would have no more than thirty thousand warriors. And that was not enough of a numerical cushion to provide any source of comfort.

Also, the Marine knew that he needed to draw the Romans out of the fort in order to engage them successfully. He was pretty sure that he would be able to do this. He was fairly sure that he could defeat them, as long as he did so before their numbers grew.

Because Nathaniel had a plan.

'Bat shit,' repeated Torkill with an incredulous look on his face.

Nathaniel nodded. 'Bat shit. Tons of it. Wagonloads of bat shit.'

'And to what end?' enquired the druid.

'We wash it,' answered Nathaniel. 'Then we sieve the water through cotton cloth and put it into large tubs. Then we allow the sun to evaporate the water off and what we get left with is a small white crystal, looks like salt. That's what I need.'

'Why?'

The Marine thought for a while before he answered. He knew that the white crystals were Potassium Nitrate or Salt Peter. He also knew that, combining one-hundred parts to twenty-three parts with finely crushed charcoal would create a basic black powder similar to gunpowder. Most people think that sulfur is necessary to make gunpowder, but the Marine had learned that the sulfur merely increased the burn rate of the black powder. The simple combination of Salt Peter and charcoal would work almost as well.

'It's magic,' he said. 'Magic crystals. Trust me.'

Torkill nodded. 'I do trust you, my lord and, if it's wagon loads of bat shit my lord wants, then it is wagon loads of bat shit my lord shall get. I shall send men to the caves forthwith.'

'And quickly,' urged Nathaniel. 'We

don't have much time.'

***

It took a full ten days to harvest the Salt Peter from the bat guano. When it was ready, Nathaniel had the corresponding amount of charcoal finely ground and then he mixed the correct quantities together.

Next, he put the black powder through a process called "Corning". Essentially, the powder was wetted with just enough water to form a dough-like consistency and then rolled into small balls and left to dry. When thoroughly dry, the balls were, once more, carefully ground into a powder. This simple process more than doubled the efficacy of the black powder, creating a super-fast burning explosive mix.

During the time that the black powder was being made, Nathaniel gathered his warriors and drilled them. He had personally scouted the land in front of the Roman fort and knew that there was only one way to win the forthcoming engagement.

He was not worried about drawing the enemy out. Simply massing his forces in front of the Romans would be the quintessential red rag to a bull. They would attack. However, the battleground in front of the fort was perfect for the Roman killing machine. Flat and large with no natural impediments it would allow the legions to perform with parade ground precision. Their formations and attack forms would be an exercise in perfection. Nathaniel had to break the formations up so that his highlanders could confront them in single combat.

He had planned and replanned and then, finally, he had put his ultimate plan to his chiefs. He did not discuss it, nor did he brook any argument.

They would do as he commanded. They all agreed.

Early the next morning Nathaniel and his thirty thousand strong host marched on the Romans. Ten thousand cavalry and twenty thousand foot soldiers.

They would outnumber the legionnaires by over ten thousand. In his heart Nathaniel knew that it was not enough.

But this was it. This was his throw of the dice. And he was feeling lucky.

CHAPTER 17

Marius couldn't believe that the savages from the other side of the wall were actually attacking the Roman fort. Well, not so much attacking, he conceded, as much as standing there in front of them and taunting them.

Many of them had pulled up their kilts to expose the nakedness underneath as they shook their genitals at the Romans and laughed.

And there were so many of the buggers. Marius had never seen so many tribesmen in one place. There must have been thirty or forty thousand of them and their screamed insults and banging of shields filled the land with a noise akin to thunder.

General Valerius had already

commanded the legates and tribunes to form up the 2nd, 6th, and 20th legions and array themselves on the battlefield.

The general had decided on the standard open field conflict battle formation, pig's head or arrow formation. The 2nd legion would be placed front and center, as they were the most elite of the three legions. They would be flanked by the 6th and the 20th. The commanders and the small amount of reserves would fall in behind them and the cavalry, such as it was, would be arrayed on either side.

There was little or no reason for any more advanced tactics. They were all confident that the battle would be short-lived and successful.

The Romans would march forwards, the enemy would charge them. They would meet in the middle. The barbarians would retreat under the pressure of the Roman killing machine. The enemy cavalry would gallop around ineffectually trying to attack the Roman shield wall and, eventually, the barbarians would turn, and the battle would become a rout.

The horns sounded, and the whistles blew. Shouted commands came rippling down the Roman line.

'Advance!'

Shields were locked and, as one, the Roman army advanced, steel shod sandals stamping in unison as they marched forward.

Nathaniel's army did not move as they faced the might of the Roman war machine bearing down on them. The Roman arrowhead formation broke into a run, covering the ground quickly, but still the highlanders remained stationary.

'We've petrified them,' shouted one of the tribunes. 'They can't even move!'

A cheer went up amongst the Romans and they struck the highlanders like a storm-wave hitting the beach.

The highlanders fought back hard but the Roman impetus overwhelmed them, and Nathaniel had the horn blow the retreat. Slowly, foot-by-foot, the highland middle gave ground. Back they went, their retreat ordered and slow.

General Valerius sounded the horn and the Roman reserves threw themselves into the fray in order to provide the final push.

It was only then that the Roman general realized that, as the highland middle had retreated, the wings of the barbarian's formation had not moved, and, in fact, the cavalry had ridden around the outside of the formation and were now ranked behind him.

The Roman army had been encircled.

However, this was not a problem. The horns blew commands and the Roman arrowhead formation pulled back into a massive square, five deep and each side containing five thousand legionnaires, inside were the commanders and the standards. There was no way that the barbarians would be able to break through this ring of steel, they would simply dash themselves to death on it as they tried.

And then Nathaniel gave his next command.

Scores of warriors ran up. There were

five sets of them and each set carried a straight young tree trunk that had been stripped of branches and bark. These trunks were then planted upright into a row of five pre-dug holes in the ground. There was a long length of rope tied around the top of each trunk and, when it was hauled on, the trunk bent backwards until the tip almost touched the ground. On the tip of each of the trunks was a leather bucket. Into each of these buckets a man placed a small wooden cask. Every cask had a short length of oil-soaked twine sticking out of it. Using torches, the lengths of twine were all lit.

And then the men let go of the ropes.

The trunks snapped back into an upright position, cracking to a stop as they reached their zenith and throwing the small wooden barrels high into the air. They arced through the sky, leaving a trail of fire as they did so, heading straight for the Roman army.

'Form a tortoise,' shouted the legates. 'Incoming boulders.'

The disciplined Romans raised their shields to protect themselves from the incoming rocks.

But they were not rocks. Every barrel contained around fifty pounds of black powder. As well as the powder, Nathaniel had rammed in two hundred caltrops to provide shrapnel. The short lengths of twine were timed to ignite the barrels while they were still in the air in order to provide an airburst, resulting in maximum damage.

The five barrels exploded almost simultaneously, the sound echoing around the valley and the hills. The ground shook and the land was filled with smoke and fire and the buzz of the red-hot caltrops as they whipped through the air, ripping through both flesh and armor. Tearing heads from bodies and limbs from torsos. The tightly formed Roman square simply disintegrated into a mêlée of shocked and disoriented individual soldiers.

Nathaniel's battle horns bayed out and the highlanders charged.

No battle is ever a foregone conclusion. The Romans were outnumbered but they were professional soldiers and they had a tried and tested command structure. The highlanders were magnificent warriors and their massive broadswords wreaked terrible havoc amongst the enemy. But, in the end, the outcome came down to individual acts of courage and heroism.

The 4th cohort 2nd legion managed to form an arrow and started to cut into the highland advance, collecting more Romans as they plunged onward, gaining in strength. An unknown highlander leaned forward in his saddle, covered his horse's eyes with his hands so that it did not falter and simply galloped into the front rank of the arrow formation, going down in a flurry of churning hooves and sandals and blades. His compatriots poured into the gap that he had formed with his sacrificial charge and they tore the formation apart.

Padraig Lancelord fought like a man demented and possessed. Already three horses had been cut down from under him, but he would spring up, find another free mount, and hurl himself back into the fray, bleeding from a multitude of cuts.

Nathaniel saw a highlander impaled by a Roman spear, only to grasp it with his free hand and drag himself down the shaft in order to get close enough to the legionnaire to behead him with a massive swing of his broadsword. He died with a smile on his lips.

Another Pictish warrior, sword broken and discarded, was savagely throttling a Roman tribune whilst at least three more Romans stabbed and cut him in an effort to stop him. Finally, he fell to the ground, his flesh almost flayed from his body. But when he fell, the tribune fell, dead, beside him.

The Marine watched as the battle waxed and waned across the field, surging and retreating. The field was awash with blood, the friable brown soil turned to a viscous, slimy, red mud that was treacherous underfoot, causing men from both sides to slip and fall.

And, as the Marine judged the battle to be finely balanced, he sounded the horn one last time and committed his reserve cavalry. Fully two thousand more fresh, heavily armed men.

It was the death knell for the mighty Romans and a shudder went through the legionnaires like a final drawing of breath.

Neither side showed any quarter and the scale of slaughter was horrific. Eventually small groups of Romans gathered together, scattered about the battlefield, and simply waited to be dispatched, some individuals simply too exhausted to raise a sword in defense.

Nathaniel, who had lost his horse to a spear thrust, came across a group of three legionnaires and he swung his axe left and right, swiftly decapitating two of them. The third jumped back and raised his sword.

'Okay, highlander,' he said. 'Let's do the dance of death.'

Nathaniel grinned and the Roman grinned back at him. They sparred for a while, steel ringing out against steel as blows were struck and parried. But it was obvious that the Marine was a superior warrior, and, after a few short minutes, the Roman held up his hand.

'Enough, highlander,' he said. 'I'm all done in. Can't hardly breathe.'

He knelt down in front of Nathaniel and took off his helmet, exposing his neck. 'Make it quick, tribesman.'

The Marine raised his axe and, as he was about to swing, Padraig shouted out.

'My lord. Stay your hand.'

The lancelord came sprinting over.

'Please, spare this man, my lord,' Padraig begged. 'He saved my life. He refused a direct order to kill me and the children that I was with. He even had to kill one of his own to do so.'

Marius looked up at Padraig. 'You look better,' he said. 'I'm glad. It's not my place to kill women and children and wounded men.'

Nathaniel lowered his axe and looked

around him. Nary a Roman was standing. The battle was over. He held his hand out to Marius and helped him to his feet.

'Rise, brave Roman. Your life is spared. Please, return to the castle with me. I shall provide you with food and shelter. After that, you will be free to do as you wish. We owe you for the life of our beloved lancelord.'

The highlander built two huge funeral pyres. One for the Romans and one for their own. The druids said the words. Mead and uisge were thrown on the flames and a herd of goats sacrificed by throwing them, alive, onto the pyres.

Then the host went home.

CHAPTER 18

All of the chiefs sat around the huge round table. And all about the table were seated more luminaries. Heroes from the battle, wives, elders, druids. Three chairs away to Nathaniel's left sat the Roman, Marius, a goblet of mead in his hand and a look of utter bemusement on his face. On the Marine's right, MacDonell, Padan and Torkill the druid.

But Nathaniel had little time for sitting. He was cruising the room. Patting backs and shaking hands. Giving credit where due and swapping stories of the great battle.

It had been a magnificent victory. A victory from which Rome would never fully recover. Twenty thousand Roman soldiers dead for the loss of only two thousand Pictish warriors. Nathaniel had left enough Romans alive to return back south to spread the news. To venture north of the wall was to court certain death.

Blood had been repaid with blood.

Nathaniel Arnthor Degeo Hogan had made sure of that.

Finally, the Marine made it back to the table and sat down exhausted in his seat. Someone shoved a goblet of uisge into his hand and he drank deep, the fiery liquid burning his throat and warming his lungs with its fragrant fire.

He looked up and saw Marius the Roman standing next to him. The legionnaire knelt down.

'King Arthur,' he said. 'I thank you for this kind invitation to sit at your round table and drink with you. It is an honor beyond all that I ever in my life expected.'

Nathaniel patted him on the back. 'No worries, Roman. And it's Arnthor, by the way, not Arthur.'

Marius smiled. 'Forgive me, king. I pronounce it in the Roman way. Arthur.

Our tongue is different. Much like our pronunciation of the name of your queen. You say Janiver, we say Guinevere. And pray tell, King Arthur, where is your queen? I would like to pay my respects and give my thanks. As well would I like to thank Padraig lancelord.'

Nathaniel stared at Marius for a full ten seconds before he spoke.

'What did you call the queen?'

'Guinevere, king.'

The world spun around Nathaniel. Colors smeared, and sound seemed to stretch out around him. Laughter and music became a dirge and a lament.

Arthur. The round table. Guinevere. Lancelord … Lancelot!

He cast his gaze around the room, searching for his friend and his queen. His lover and his right-hand man.

Torkill the druid grasped the Marine by the shoulder. 'My lord,' he said. 'What is wrong? You have gone as pale as death.'

Nathaniel grabbed his axe from his belt as he sprang to his feet and ran from the room. Torkill, Marius, and Padan followed him.

He sprinted down corridors, throwing open doors, almost tripping and falling in his haste. Grunting as he ran, like a gut-shot animal.

Finally, he came to Padraig's room and he kicked the door open.

Entwined on the bed were the two of them. Their naked flesh burnished gold by the firelight, the sounds of their passion cutting through the air like daggers.

Slicing into Nathaniel's heart. Wounding him. Rending him.

A cry of mortal agony escaped from his lips and he stood rooted to the spot.

Janiver gasped and pulled up the bedclothes to cover her nakedness.

Padraig walked over to Nathaniel and fell to his knees in front of him, tears streamed down his face.

'Forgive me, my lord,' he gasped. 'I

could not stop myself. By the gods, I tried. I tried so hard.'

He pulled his long hair from the back of his neck. 'Please, lord. Strike me down now. Kill me.'

Nathaniel stood, panting with rage and passion, his chest rising and falling like a set of bellows.

And then he raised his axe high and brought it down … stopping as it touched Padraig's neck.

'No,' he whispered. 'You will live. Death is too good for you.'

The Marine turned and ran from the castle and into the fields. He ran from the pain. He ran from the horror. And behind him followed Torkill and Padan.

He fell to his knees and raised his axe above him.

The night skies burst open with a flash of color and a bolt of lightning crashed down from the heavens and struck the axe.

And the druid cried out in dismay and terror. For The Forever Man had gone.

Nathaniel Arnthor Degeo Hogan, King Arthur—was no more.

CHAPTER 19

Tad picked up the hare that he had just killed and placed it into a sack tied to his belt. That made four. Enough for the day. He would dress them when he got home. Every bit would be used, from flesh to fur to entrails.

As the little big man walked back towards his cottage he kept an eye out for wolves. There had been a vast increase in both their numbers and their size of late and it was a foolish man who didn't keep his eyes peeled for them. Especially when out alone.

He approached the standing stone with Nathaniel's mark on it and, as he always did, remembered the day that the Marine had simply disappeared into thin air, leaving not a trace behind, save some footprints in the snow.

After the Marine's almost magical disappearance in front of so many witnesses the standing stone itself had become a place of reverence. Almost an object of worship. Many people went so far as to leave offerings at the foot of the stone. Fruit, bunches of flowers. At times a chicken or rabbit.

Tad noticed that, this morning, someone had left something more substantial. It looked like a pile of clothing. Perhaps a blanket.

It was only when he got closer that he saw it was actually a person, lying huddled up in a fetal position at the foot of the stone. He was wearing a great kilt, a rough leather tunic and a pair of thick sandals. His face was covered by a mane of dark hair.

Lying, in the snow next to him, was an axe. An axe that Tad knew only too well.

He ran forward and knelt next to the body, pushing the hair back to see his features.

And, unbidden, tears sprang from his

eyes and ran freely down his cheeks. The man looked slightly older, perhaps more careworn and haggard than touched by age. He was scarred, and his hair and beard looked like they had not seen a barber for at least a year, but there was no mistaking it.

Nathaniel Hogan was back.

***

The Marine sat at the table. His face was drawn and pale. His eyes haunted. Tad had dragged him back to his place and laid him on a pallet to sleep. He had slept for two days and now, finally awake, he was drinking some hot rabbit soup that Tad had made.

He had not yet spoken, and Tad had not pushed him to.

Finally, Nathaniel finished the soup. He cleared his throat.

'You look different,' he said to Tad. The dwarf nodded.

'Aye. So do you.'

'You look older,' continued the Marine.

'Your hair is longer,' answered Tad.

Nathaniel leant forward and touched the hair at Tad's temples.

'You're going gray.'

Tad nodded again. 'Aye. Time will do that to a man.'

Nathaniel looked baffled. 'How? I mean … how long has it been?'

'How long do you think?' asked Tad

The Marine shrugged. 'A year. Maybe a little more.'

Tad smiled. 'Try twenty-two years, my friend. When you left I was a young man. Now I am forty-four years old. Hence the gray hair.'

'Where's Gruff. Gruff McGunn?'

Tad shook his head. 'Dead. He died in a skirmish with the Orcs some twelve years back. A lot has changed since you left, Nate. A hell of a lot.'

Nathaniel squeezed his eyes shut. Nothing made sense. He had no anchor with which to fasten his reality to the world. He had no center. His world was awash with uncertainty. A wave of self-pity washed over him, but he crushed it before it had a chance to grow. For that way lay madness.

'Tell me all,' he said to Tad. 'Leave nothing out.'

And so, he did.

Over the last twenty years the Fair-Folk had expanded both in influence and numbers. It was guesstimated that there were in excess of three million Orcs, and around two million goblins. Numbers regarding trolls were unsubstantiated and, as for the actual Fair-Folk themselves, estimates varied between one hundred thousand to as high as half a million.

It had been made law that humans carried a pass with them at all times and travel between counties was forbidden without express permission from the Fair-Folk or one of their minions.

As with any totalitarian occupation, many humans had defected completely to the side of the Fair-Folk, becoming either subservient lackeys or, worse, fully participating allies with all of the benefits thereof. Those humans wore gray uniforms and were given first choice, after the Fair-Folk, of both housing and food

Collectively they were referred to as members of HAS or the Human Advisory Service.

Many humans were forced into labor on farms, mines, and lumber operations whilst Fair-Folk and HAS members lived in luxury.

Whilst the lowlands of Scotland had a few Fair-Folk supporters living there, the Highlands, with the new harsh weather patterns, were almost free of them, peopled by the less accepting, old-fashioned humans. The almost constant freezing temperatures, lack of arable land and general savagery of the people kept the Fair-Folk and their minions out.

And, as such, it was punishable, by

death, for any human to venture north of Hadrian's Wall without written permission of the ruling classes.

'On the plus side,' said Tad. 'The human population is, once again, on the increase.'

Nathaniel shook his head. 'Jesus, I can't get my mind around this. The human race has been taken over by the pig-people?'

'Well, not the pig-people as such,' answered Tad. 'The Fair-Folk. They're the boss of the pig-people or Orcs. Also, the goblins. The Fair-Folk are like us. Well, like you, I suppose. Tall, fair-haired, good-looking. Male models all of them. The females are seldom seen and, when they are, they tend to be covered. Veils and crap. Sort of like Muslims. Personally, I don't think that even the most rabid of HAS members would actually allow themselves to be subjugated by Orcs. But, whatever one says about the Fair-Folk, they've got class.'

Tad got up and went to fetch a couple

of mugs and a bottle of uisge. He poured a stiff measure for each of them.

'There's something else,' he said. 'Something really weird. Not actually sure how to tell you, so I'll just do it.'

He stood up again and went through to his bedroom, returning with a large, hardcover book. He placed it on the table in front of Nathaniel.

The book was leather-bound and, on the cover, etched in gold leaf was the title. "Myths and legends of Scotland."

Tad flicked it open and ran through a few pages before stopping at a full color print of a detailed, oil painted, portrait.

The person in the portrait was, absolutely and undeniably, Nathaniel. And it was the Marine as he looked at that very moment. The artist had captured the haunted look in his eyes, the length of hair and beard. Even the leather tunic and the tartan of the great kilt were identical. In the foreground of the picture lay Nathaniel's axe.

Underneath the caption read. "King

Arthur of the Picts." Nathaniel stared at the picture.

'How long has this been around?' he asked.

Tad shrugged. 'Forever, apparently.'

'Yes,' continued the Marine. 'But was it around forever before I went away or was it only around forever since then?'

Again, Tad shrugged.

'I think that I always remember it. Whatever. Is it true?'

Nathaniel glanced through the write up. Reading quickly.

He nodded. 'Basically. Except for the part where a boat came and took me away to the lady of the lake. As far as I know I got zapped by lightning and ended up back here. There was a round table, a castle. Lancelot … bloody prick. I see that there's no mention of the Holy Grail.'

Tad raised an eyebrow. 'No, not sure what you're talking about. You found the Holy Grail?'

'No,' denied Nathaniel. 'The other

King Arthur. The one before I went back and messed it all up. Anyway—it doesn't matter. I see that it says here that I'll come back when I am most needed in order to lead the clans against a new enemy?'

Tad nodded.

'Well then,' said Nathaniel. 'That should help. As long as I can convince them that I'm the long dead legendary King Arthur come back to help fight the Fair-Folk and not some psycho nutcase with porridge for brains.'

'We'll find a way,' encouraged Tad.

'What if I don't want to?' asked the Marine. 'What if I simply do not bloody care anymore?'

Tad smiled. 'We'll find a way,' he repeated and poured another mug-full of uisge for the Marine.

CHAPTER 20

Tad pulled the saddle cinch tight.

'Are you sure about this?' he asked.

'Definitely,' affirmed Nathaniel as he mounted his horse. 'If I've been gone for over twenty years, first I need to take a bit of a tour of the country. Get a bit of firsthand knowledge etcetera.'

Tad grunted as he threw another two full saddlebags over the back of the packhorse that they were taking with them.

'What's that?' asked Nathaniel. 'I thought that we'd already packed all of the food and stuff.'

'Goods to trade,' replied Tad. 'Told you that things have changed. Can't just live off the land now. Well, you can, but you also need to be able to trade for goods, places to stay, and so on.'

'So, what you got?'

'Small knives. A few pots and pans. Goblets. Some bottles of uisge.'

The dwarf clambered onto his horse, still holding the long reins attached to the packhorse. He tied them loosely to the back of his saddle and they set off. He had left his cottage unlocked and had allowed one of the village bachelors to stay in it, hoping that at least he would keep the damp out.

They had no real plan of action. Nathaniel figured that he wanted to travel to London and then back. Firstly, they had to sneak across the wall. Then, somehow, they needed to find a member of HAS so that they could obtain the requisite paperwork. Tad had been assured by other travelers that it was pretty much a given that any member of HAS was imminently corruptible and a few bottles of highland uisge would purchase any and all certifications needed.

It took them four days to ride from Tomintoul to Wardrew Wood.

When they got to the woods they used the cover of the trees to cross the remnants of Hadrian's Wall at that point and then, under the cover of darkness, made their way to the village of Chapleburn where they traded a set of knives for dinner, bed, breakfast, and stabling for their mounts.

The next morning, they rose early, ate well and, after asking directions, set off to the local HAS office on foot.

Chapelburn was a large village. Before the pulse it probably housed around seven thousand souls. Now it was closer to three thousand and more than half of those were aliens. Long armed goblins and pig-faced Orcs being the norm

Nathaniel, who had at this point only heard of Orcs and goblins, could not stop staring.

'Bugger me,' he whispered to Tad. 'People had explained what they looked like but, Jesus, they are plug-ugly, aren't they?'

'Which ones' Asked Tad.

'Both,' answered Nathaniel. 'The pig-faces and the goblins.'

'Stop staring,' said Tad. 'You're like a child. You're attracting attention. Act normal.'

Nathaniel tore his eyes away from the shambling monstrosities and tried to look as if the sight of them was an everyday occurrence to him. But he couldn't stop himself shuddering involuntarily every now and then.

After a couple of wrong turns, they came to the address that they were looking for. A run-down Georgian mansion with a front door that opened directly onto the street.

Nathaniel rapped on it, using the knocker.

They heard footsteps shuffling closer and, eventually, the door was opened by a short, weedy looking man with a huge pot belly that even his well-cut gray uniform failed to conceal.

He threw his arm out in a fascist salute. 'Hail, good people,' he greeted.

'Hail, worthy human,' greeted Tad back.

Nathaniel stared at the man for a few seconds and then burst out laughing.

'You gotta be kidding me,' he said. 'Bloody Hail and the Hitler salute. What the hell. No ways.'

Tad grabbed the Marine by the arm and pulled him down to his level. 'Listen, Nate,' he urged. 'Don't. These buggers take the whole HAS thing real serious. You don't have to salute but you must refer to him as a worthy human. Do it or we're screwed before we begin. Also— apologize.'

Nathaniel took a deep breath and stood straight. He stared at the pot-bellied man and whipped out a salute that would have brought tears to Goebbels' eyes.

'Hail and greetings, worthy human,' he barked out in his best Marine master sergeant parade ground voice. The greeting boomed into the house and echoed around the rooms. 'I must apologize, worthy human,' continued Nathaniel at top volume. 'I was filled with excitement at actually meeting a worthy human member of HAS and I was overcome, hence my apparent rudeness. Hail,' he boomed again.

Tad kicked him surreptitiously in the shin and whispered. 'All right. Enough already. Slow down.'

The man smiled at Nathaniel and nodded. 'You are forgiven, young man,' he said. 'I understand. But please relax; we worthy humans are not to be feared—only respected. Come in, the two of you. How may I help?'

'We are traveling traders,' said Tad as they followed the man down the dingy corridor and into his office. 'We live fairly locally, a mile or so outside of the hamlet of Truebough. We look for permits to travel to London and back in order to trade.'

'And what goods do you trade in?' asked the official. Tad had come well prepared for this and he opened his leather saddlebag and started to place goods on the desk in front of the man. Two bottles of golden uisge, a set of three, honed, bright, steel throwing knives, a short sword, and a necklace of semi-precious stones.

'Please, worthy human, allow us to make a humble gift of these goods so that you may make yourself aware of both our products and their quality.'

The official stared at the row of goods for a while and then he lifted one of the bottles of uisge.

'I have friends who are very fond of this,' he said. 'It would be nice if I could make them each a gift of a bottle.'

'Of course,' agreed Tad. 'How many friends, worthy human?'

'Four.'

Tad pulled another five bottles out of his bag.

'Please accept these with our compliments, worthy human. I hope that your friends will be well pleased. The uisge is over ten years old.'

The official smiled and removed some

papers from a drawer in his desk. He scrawled some words onto the scroll and then, tongue between his teeth with concentration, he applied his wax seal to the bottom of the paper.

'Here,' he pushed the paper across. 'Travel between here and London. You may not proceed more than five miles off the accepted route, nor may you proceed more than five miles past the southern limits of the city itself.

He stood up and threw out another fascist salute. 'All hail.'

Tad and Nathaniel stood and saluted back. 'Hail to you, worthy human,' they shouted in unison.

'That will be all,' said the official as he led them to the front door and showed them out.

As they walked down the street Nathaniel mumbled. 'Stupid dick. Hail, my ass.'

Tad laughed. 'Told you there had been changes.' Nathaniel shook his head. 'It's not only that,' he said.

'Look at this place.' He gestured around him. The concrete of the pavements and the blacktop roads were full of potholes and puddles. Raw sewage flowed down the storm drains and the place smelled like an open toilet. The humans walking about the place all had looks of dejection and exhaustion on their careworn faces. Clothes, on the whole, were shabby and re-patched or badly homemade.

A bucket of excrement, thrown from a second-floor window, splashed onto the pavement next to Nathaniel, barely missing him and dotting his boots with brown speckles.

'Why are people living like this?' he asked Tad. 'Why don't they leave the villages and live off the land?'

'Because they can't,' replied Tad. 'Don't forget. There used to be almost seventy-five million people living in the United Kingdom. A year after the pulse that had shrunk to seven or eight. People guess that it's around eight again. The ones that survived did so mainly through dumb luck. Your average bloke doesn't know how to live off the land. Jesus, man. Some of the city kids thought that milk came from a machine and pasta was grown on pasta bushes. Also, you have to appreciate, things started to wear out mighty quickly. You wash clothes and bedding without soap means that you have to really bash your washing with a rock or something, bedding, linen, clothes. Everything started to seriously wear out after about ten years. When the Fair-Folk cobbled together some semblance of order, people flocked to the towns and villages under their control. There was security, a guarantee of sustenance. Roof over their heads. Okay, they had to live like peasants, or worse, but at least they stopped dying.'

'I'd rather die,' said Nathaniel.

'Would you?' asked Tad. 'Really? Well I for one hope to hell that I never have to make that choice. Come on, let's get our horses and blow this cesspit.'

CHAPTER 21

Janeka stood upright and stretched her back, then she leant against the hoe for a while, feeling and looking twenty years older than her true age of forty-two. The last few years had been tough. Real tough. But she was alive, she was relatively healthy. The Fair-Folk allowed her, and the rest of the workers, enough calories every day to live. She had a roof over her head at night and there were no bandit problems.

She counted the days and years up in her head. It had been six years since her sister, Adalyn had died. Taken from her by some nasty little tumor. Some filthy cancer that ate away at her insides, leaving her a wasted, pain-wracked facsimile of her former self.

Gramma Higgins was still going

strong at eighty-four years of age. Although she had neither official title nor position on the farm, or the collective as the Fair-Folk called it, nothing of note was done without running it by Gramma first. Not even the Orcs did anything of note without telling the old lady. And, if by chance they did, she would take them to one side and give them a stern telling off, berating them for upwards of twenty minutes at least, her strident Jamaican patois ringing out across the farm.

But the actual official human in charge, third in the hierarchy after Djedi, the Fair-Folk leader and Pog, the Orc garrison commander, was Milly.

Worthy human and fanatical member of HAS, she was more alien than human. Never missing a chance to preach to all, how the Fair-Folk had saved humanity. How the world had totally gone to shit before the Orcs and goblins had joined with the humans to steer them back onto the path.

Where Janeka saw subjugation, Milly saw a partnership. Where Janeka saw control, Milly saw guidance.

Twenty-nine years of age and stunningly beautiful. Tall, long auburn hair that tumbled in tight curls to below her shoulders, eyes of burned hazel, and the body of a professional athlete. She could outride most men and, in any close physical combat, could more than hold her own.

Janeka had helped bring Milly up, seeing her grow from little girl to the self-assured adult fanatic that she was now. Once almost sisters, Milly now treated Janeka with cool politeness and insisted on being addressed as worthy human and saluted in the fascist way. The Jamaican girl supposed that she should hate Milly. Despise her for her fickleness. But she simply didn't have the energy. Merely living was all that she could manage. Grubbing in the dirt to fulfill the Fair-Folk's agricultural quotas, mechanical mastication of food to impart energy, sleep in order to recharge her exhausted body and then more dirt grubbing. It was life … but it was not living.

'Hey,' one of the goblin supervisors called out to her in its guttural voice. 'No sleeping on hoe. Work.'

She took a deep breath and went back to turning the soil.

***

Nathaniel was amazed. The farm was vast. At least ten times larger than the burgeoning little settlement that he had left a little over a year ago.

And then he had to remind himself that it had actually been over twenty years. Twenty years of concerted, planned growth using forced human labor.

From his vantage point on the top of the hill he could see that the fifty acres of before had now become over two thousand acres of well laid out crops. He could see potatoes, pumpkins, cabbages, and turnips. Crops that could withstand the vagaries of the post- pulse weather patterns. Closer to the main living area were sheds containing laying hens and, to the side, what looked like pig-pens.

They had already been vetted by a team of guards. A mixture of Orcs, goblins, and worthy humans. Their paperwork had held up and they were given permission to stay overnight and to trade some of their knives for jams and preserved fruits. Uisge was forbidden but they were allowed to keep it as long as they did not bring it out of their saddlebags.

They had asked for directions to the inn and an Orc had given them directions to what he called the guesting area. When they arrived, they found it to be a large, drafty barn. Mean, bare bunks lined up along the walls. There was no fire; no windows and the main doors did not shut. But it seemed relatively waterproof and it was free, although Tad maintained that, even at that price, it was a rip-off.

Next to the barn was a lean-to for the horses. Hay was provided and although they asked one of the goblins, there did not seem to be any oats. The goblin was so nervous of the horses that he kept moving away from them whenever they approached. As a result, they decided to tie the horses up in the lean-to and they buried their saddlebags under the hay, trusting that the horses would discourage any opportunist thievery. They took with them a few sets of knives, both combat and cooking.

As it happened they had nothing to worry about. The Fair-Folk had deemed the theft of any property illegal, and so, as with all illegal actions, it was punishable by hanging. Human malingering, showing a lack of respect to either the Fair-Folk or their minions, or to a worthy human, or raising a hand in violence against same also constituted a capital offence. In fact, humans were regularly beaten for minor transgressions.

The Fair-Folk and the worthy humans considered this to be tough but reasonable. Worthy humans such as Milly were always sprouting sayings such as, "Self-respect is the fruit of discipline," or "Discipline is the bridge between goals and accomplishment."

After an hour or so of wandering around and asking directions they found the central storage offices.

Both Nathaniel and Tad were amazed at the vast amounts of bureaucracy that seemed to be generated by the Fair-Folk's rules. There was an officer for everything. Planting, reaping, preserving. Storage, accommodation, food allowances, maintenance, safety.

The place reminded the Marine of the old Soviet Union that he had studied in history classes. Gray and dour and inefficient. The people worn and listless but alive.

The central storing offices were run by a goblin and three worthy humans. Tad and Nathaniel were sat opposite a worthy human and they took out their knives. Tad went into his sales pitch, showing the quality of the blades, the leather handles. Promoting the balance and superiority of the craftsmanship.

When he had finished the worthy

human simply said. 'Cooking knives get five jars of fruit preserve. Military blades under six inches get seven jars.'

Tad assumed an air of amazement. 'Of course, worthy human,' he said. 'But look at these blades. Bright steel. The best leather handles. Feel how sharp they are.'

'Cooking knives, five jars. Military blades under six inches, seven jars. Take or leave it. I don't care which.'

'Just give him the blades,' said Nathaniel.

Tad, a disappointed look on his face, slid across the selection of knives. The human disappeared into the warehouse and came back with two large sacks.

'Here,' he said as he placed them onto the table. 'One hundred and twenty-three jars of fruit preserve, assorted.'

He glanced over their shoulders. There were two more tradesmen waiting.

'Next,' he flicked his hand at Tad and Nathaniel. 'Go.'

The next two traders shuffled up to the

desk. 'Tin plates and mugs. Looking for pickled and preserved vegetables.'

'Tin mugs, two jars of pickled vegetables, assorted. Tin plates, three jars.' responded the store man.

The Marine and the dwarf walked out, each carrying a sack.

'Bloody ridiculous,' fumed Tad. 'It makes no sense. If I'd offered him some rusty old piece of crap cutlery I would have got the same price as I did for top quality stuff.'

Nathaniel grinned. 'Centralized economy. That's how it works. I don't know why you're so chipped off. I mean, we aren't actually here to trade, are we?'

'That's not the point,' argued Tad. 'It doesn't make sense. It offends me. Who decides what is worth what?'

Nate shrugged. 'Don't know. Some clueless worthy human. Who cares?'

Tad sniffed. 'Idiots.'

They turned the corner into the street that the guesting barn was in and Tad almost walked straight into someone.

'Sorry,' he said.

'Watch where you're going,' the person replied. 'It's not a race, you know.'

Tad froze, staring. 'Janeka?'

She stared back at him.

'Tad?' She went down on one knee and threw her arms around the small man. The two of them stood in silence for a while. Holding each other. Then Janeka looked up. 'It can't be,' she said. 'Nathaniel?' She stood up and hugged him.

'Jesus, Nate,' she continued. 'You look like you haven't aged a day. Hair's longer. A few more scars. How is that possible?'

Nathaniel laughed. 'Clean living, abstinence, and a vegan diet,' he answered. 'No, seriously,' he continued. 'Is there some place we can talk in private? I can explain.'

She nodded. 'I stay with Gramma. It's just the two of us in the house.'

'Where's Adalyn?' asked Tad.

Janeka shook her head. 'Gone. The cancer ate her up some six years back. But Gramma's still strong. Most people have to share rooms but they all treat Gramma special. Come.'

They followed Janeka past the guesting barn, through some narrow alleys and, finally, to a small stand-alone house at the end of a short, quiet street.

'Hey,' said Nathaniel. 'How come this street isn't covered in shit and stuff like all of the others?'

Janeka laughed.

'Gramma don't allow it. Long drops out the back. Rubbish taken and dumped elsewhere. If you disobey then she comes around to your house and talks at you. Nobody wants that. Even the Orcs treat Gramma with respect. Actually, the goblins are petrified of her and the worthy humans all call her ma'am. Except for Milly, of course.'

'Milly's still around?' asked Nathaniel eagerly.

Janeka nodded. 'We'll talk about that

later. Come on.' She opened the door and showed them in. 'Gramma,' she shouted. 'Visitors.'

'I's in da kitchen, child. Making tisane.'

Janeka led the way down the corridor and into the kitchen. It was a fairly large room. Painted bright blue. An open fire in the one wall and a wood stove in the corner. Both were going, and the room was as hot as a summer's day. Gramma was throwing some herbs into a large battered teapot and stirring it with a wooden spoon.

She looked up at the visitors and froze.

'Lordy be,' she said. 'If it ain't the little big man and the Marine.'

Both Nathaniel and Tad gave the old lady a hug. She took some more mugs from the cupboard and poured tisane for all, sweetening it with honey.

Then she sat down and stared long and hard at Nathaniel. 'You ain't aged none,' she said.

'You look the same as well, Gramma,' retorted Nate. 'Bullshine,' Gramma said. 'I look all of my eighty plus years. You ain't aged at all. Not a day. Your hair got longer, and someone cut you face some. So, it's true what we thought back then … you is immortal.'

'Not sure, Gramma,' answered Nathaniel. 'I went away, but only for a year. When I got back more than twenty years had passed.'

Gramma raised an eyebrow. 'Tell me about it, child.'

So, Nathaniel did, and the story took a while in the telling. Tad broke out a bottle of the forbidden uisge and the four of them drank as the story unfolded.

Nathaniel finished with his return home and Tad's discovering him at the foot of the standing stone.

Gramma nodded. 'I know de story of King Arthur. I tells you, that Guinevere was one conniving bitch.'

Nate shrugged. 'I loved her, Gramma.'

'What you know about love?' questioned the old lady. 'You but a child.'

Gramma poured herself another shot if uisge. 'You know summat, Marine. I'm not sure now if I always knew dat story or if I only always knew it now dat you told it to me.'

'I remember a different story,' admitted Nathaniel. 'There was a holy grail and there were knights in armor. Also, a sword called Excalibur.'

Everyone else at the table shook their heads. 'Doesn't ring any bells,' said Janeka. 'The King Arthur that I knew was always king of the Picts.'

'Me too,' admitted Gramma and Tad.

'Well that's my story, Gramma, now, talk to me about Milly,' said the Marine.

Janeka looked at her feet and Gramma gave a huge sigh before she spoke

'That, Nathaniel my boy, is a story that is not as happy as it should be.'

The Marine pulled another bottle of golden spirit from the pocket of his long coat, cracked the seal and refilled Gramma's mug.

'Not many are, Gramma,' said Nathaniel. 'But they all need to be told, nonetheless.'

The old lady nodded her agreement, took a slug of whisky, and started to talk.

'When you and Tad left the farm all those years ago, Milly hated you for it,' said Gramma. 'Especially you, Nate. She felt abandoned, betrayed. Alone.'

'She had you guys,' argued the Marine. 'And I did it for her own good. Life in the wilds was no life for a young girl.'

'Grown-up thinking,' said Gramma. 'All dat mean nothing to a little girl. Her parents died, you took her on, you up and left. I's not blaming you or discussing right or wrong,' continued Gramma. 'I's simply telling a story, so shuts up and listen.'

'Sorry, Gramma. Go ahead.'

'Dem early times was tough. Hand-to-mouth existence, living mainly on potatoes. Constant attack by roving bands of bandits. But the defenses dat you had put together and the system of patrols you set up, dey worked real good. After a year the bandits got to know, don't attack the farm, it'll only end badly. Until a man by the name of Curtis O'Reilly. Irishman. He puts his self together a gang of his own and then proceeds to gather all the other bandits together. Collected his self up about sixty of them. One day, just before sun up he hits the farm, but we's ready 'cause we had scouts and guards and all dat stuff you told us to do. So, Curtis and his merry men, they takes an almighty beating. We killed nigh on fifty of the assholes. But they managed to break into the inner defenses before we beats them back. They killed seven of us and, on the way out, they grabbed Milly. Kidnapped her. Soon as we found out we put together a force of mounted men and went after her. Caught up wid them the next day. Brought them back to the farm, cut their stomachs open and then strung them up by the river to die slowly. People came to watch.'

'Wow,' said Nathaniel. 'Bit harsh.'

Gramma shook her head. 'No. We was lenient on the mothers. They raped that little girl. Not one or two of them. They all did. She didn't talk for six months. Walked around like a zombie. Then de Fair-Folk came. With their battle Orcs and goblin archers and trolls and such stuff. No one ever attacked de farm again. How could they? Them Orcs might be pig-ugly, but they can fight like the devil. Wasn't long and de only bandits in de area was buried under a butt load of soil. They brought order, law, and food. Milly loved them for that. They did for her what we humans couldn't. And they never gone and left her neither. Given choice, dat girl will take the side of the Fair-Folk above her fellow man. She be well and truly a convert. She is a full on worthy human.'

Nathaniel took a deep breath. 'I need to see her. To talk to her.'

Gramma shook her head. 'No, my child, you do not. For the right or the wrong of it, that little girl hates your guts. If you hadn't left, she wouldn't have been raped. You see? All the bad crap that happened to her … it be your fault, Marine. It be all your fault.'

Nathaniel Hogan was not yet thirty years of age. Yet he had fought and conquered the Romans at Hadrian's Wall. He had become a king. He had been pinned down by sniper fire in the never-ending war in Afghanistan. He had survived the fall of man and traveled across time and space. He had gained immortality and, with it, had taken on a geas that now controlled his life.

But what Gramma had just told him affected him like nothing that he had experienced before. She was correct, if he had not left, then Milly would have been safe. He had abandoned her to follow some unexplained obsession that kept pulling him north. He could have … he should have, taken her with him.

***

Tad and Nathaniel left early the next

morning, just before sunrise. The Marine had not seen Milly, but he had promised to pop back in on Janeka and Gramma on his way back—if he did come back.

Their saddlebags were heavier now that they had over a hundred jars of fruit preserve but they would trade them for something lighter at some stage. Neither of them was that bothered about it. After all, the whole trading thing was merely a cover and a way to enable them to live when they were unable to live off the land itself.

The two men rode in silence, heading in a vaguely southerly direction. Tad didn't push the Marine for conversation. He knew that he was struggling to come to terms with what Gramma had told him the night before.

Eventually Tad spoke.

'It wasn't your fault,' he said.

'Yes, it was,' replied Nathaniel.

There was nothing that the little big man could say in return.

CHAPTER 22

Pawah Patenemheb, ambassador to the Fair-Folk and assistant to commander Ammon turned up his concentration and brought the full power of his glamour onto the human sitting opposite him.

Waves of coercion boiled off him as his magiks altered human perception. This glamoring ensured that they all saw him as a six foot, blonde, square-jawed, blue-eyed Adonis. As opposed to a four foot high, domed-headed, bald, rubber-skinned alien.

The Fair-Folk had still not allowed their true selves to be perceived by the humans. They realized that control was far easier when they looked less alien and more akin to the widely accepted norm of the generic Alpha male cliché.

As well as changing his visual

perception, Pawah was also using his coercion in an attempt to subtly control the human's mind. To sway him over to his way of thinking.

But it did little to help. Axel Bainbridge, ex-captain Queen's Guards, was from the sort of English upper-class family that was naturally immune to all forms of mental coercion or blandishments. His rock-solid sense of enlightenment, courtesy of Eton, one thousand years of inbreeding and being a member of Her Majesty's Army, combined to create a man whose self-confidence and self-belief were as solid and as unmoving as a rock.

'But, Captain,' said Pawah. 'You must understand, all that we, as the Fair-Folk do, is for your own good. We provide protection, a market for your wares and freedom from worry.'

'You do nothing of the sort, ambassador,' retorted Axel. 'We at the abbey, protect ourselves. We produce superior products and find no difficulty in trading them for their actual worth. If we allowed ourselves to be enveloped by the Fair-Folk and their restrictive policies, it would devalue our products and services and give us nothing in return.'

'But, Captain,' continued Pawah. 'I have been told to advise you that we must insist on your full cooperation.'

'Well then ambassador,' replied Axel. 'I must advise you, with all due respect, to go screw yourselves.'

'Captain, there is no need for such aggression.'

'I disagree, ambassador. I think that aggression is the only thing that you Fair-Folk understand. Let me lay this out for you. I control an army of six hundred horses, five hundred archers and eight hundred foot. On top of that we maintain a citizen force of another two thousand auxiliaries. All told, about four thousand warriors. Now, I know that, compared to your forces, we are relatively insubstantial, however, if you push us, we will attack you. Eventually you will almost beat us. And I say almost, because aside from my standard forces, I have a force of five hundred guerillas.'

'I am not familiar with that word,' interrupted the ambassador.

'Well then, let me acquaint you,' said Axel. 'If you defeat our conventional army, my guerillas will split into groups of between three and five. A mixture of male and female, young and old. Indistinguishable from the normal population. They are then tasked with destroying anything to do with the Fair-Folk. Food supplies, sabotage of buildings, poisoning water supplies. Forever and ever and ever. You see, we cannot win. But then, ultimately, neither can you.'

Pawah thought for a while.

'That is not logical. If you simply acceded to our suggestions, then all would be fine.'

'Look, ambassador, I am not going to even attempt to explain to you how wrong you are. Suffice to say, be happy with the current status quo. Things are working. We humans are not a logical species, we are driven by things other than mere food and shelter.'

Pawah shook his head. 'I disagree. Many of you are.'

Axel grinned. 'True. But not all. And you would do well to remember that. I won't show you out, ambassador,' finished Axel. 'After all, you know the way.'

The ambassador stood up and left the room. Outside, his two battle Orc bodyguards walked beside him as he left the building.

Axel opened one of the desk drawers, took out a cigar and lit from the burning candle on his desktop. The private door to his office opened and his wife, Janice, walked in. He smiled at her, amazed, as he was every day, that this beautiful, bright woman had chosen to stay with him. Over twenty years ago she had come across him, wounded, his face burned, his left eye missing and he on the very verge of death. And she had saved him. They had both been given shelter by the kind professor in charge of the abbey school that formed the base of what was now one of the biggest occupied towns in England.

Leadership had passed on to Axel some twelve years ago and the professor, although still sprightly and young for his years, spent most of his time either napping or arguing with Father O'Hara about anything and everything, while the town priest spent most of his time in a constant state of jovial inebriation.

'The ambassador still giving you a tough time?' asked Janice.

'As always,' agreed Axel. 'We disturb their sense of order. Also, commander Ammon wants to place an Orc battle group inside the abbey lands. As well as that he wanted to put one of his worthy humans into my office as an "assistant." I rejected his offer most forcefully. The ambassador made a few veiled threats, but I called his bluff. I'm not sure what worries them so much.'

'I suspect that they think that you may lead some sort of revolution against them,' ventured Janice.

Axel snorted. 'Hardly likely. Even if I wanted to, which I don't, humanity isn't ready for it. Say what you like about the Fair-Folk, they have enforced some sort of order into what was an ungovernable world.'

'I agree,' said Janice. 'But at what cost? People subsist, but no more than that. The lion's share of food and materials go to the Fair-Folk and their minions, or to the so-called, worthy humans.'

'Basic socialism,' said Axel. 'Give the people just enough to survive but not enough to feed their ambition. Everybody is equal except for those who aren't. In this case the Fair-Folk and the worthies. Still, not my problem, I have the abbey to run and that'll do me fine. Anyway, the ambassador and his retinue are staying at one of our guest houses. He has another meeting scheduled with me tomorrow morning. Apparently wants to discuss trading quotas, prices, and such. It's going to be another disappointing meeting for him and a frustrating one for me while I try to explain the concept of free-trade and letting the market decide the price and production of goods.' There was a knock on the office door. 'Come in,' said Axel.

A man entered, middle-aged, wearing leather trousers and a cotton shirt. On his belt were a sword and a dagger. On his shoulder, a white star above crossed lances denoting that he was a gate-guard.

He saluted. 'Captain. Two men arrived an hour ago. They insist on seeing you.'

Axel shook his head. 'Tell them no. Ask them to see Lieutenant Swires. He can handle it.'

'They were very insistent, sir,' continued the guard. 'The one said to tell you that he's an old friend. He calls himself "Marine Master Sergeant Hogan."'

Axel raised an eyebrow. He remembered the Marine very well. He had met him over twenty years ago and he was the most awesome fighting machine that the captain had ever come across. The Marine had, almost single-handedly, killed over fifty people in one battle. And then, after saving the abbey, he had simply disappeared. Rumors said that he had gone north. But, since then, rumor mentioned only his death. No two stories matched but everyone seemed to agree that he was gone. Axel was very pleased to hear differently.

He nodded to the gate-guard.

'Send the two of them in. And, while you're about it, go and fetch the professor and father O'Hara. They'll definitely want to see him.'

The guard saluted and dashed off.

A few minutes later he returned and ushered Nathaniel and Tad in.

'I have alerted the professor and the father,' the guard said to Axel. 'And here are your visitors.'

He closed the door behind him as he left.

Nathaniel stepped forward and held out his hand. 'Axel.'

The captain hesitated and then he proffered his hand in welcome. 'Sorry, Nathaniel. It's just that … I … you haven't aged.'

Janice came forward and gave the Marine a hug. 'It's good to see you again, Nate,' she said. 'It's been a long time.'

Nathaniel nodded. 'Longer for some than for others.' He gestured at Tad.

'This is my friend, Tad. We met a long time ago, sort of.'

Tad waved a hello.

'You're sounding very cryptic, Nathaniel,' said Axel. 'Care to explain?'

'Your man said that the prof and O'Hara were coming. If you don't mind, I'll wait and then I only have to tell the story once. It's rather long and complicated.'

On cue the door opened, and the two older men walked in. Father O'Hara immediately gathered Nathaniel up in a great bear hug, kissing him soundly on the cheek and then ruffling his long hair. 'Dere you are, me boyo,' he boomed. 'Twenty years on and as young and as ugly as ever.'

'As are you, Father,' replied

Nathaniel.

The professor greeted the Marine with a little more decorum, shaking his hand vigorously for almost a minute. Obviously as pleased as the father to see him but more reticent in his behavior.

Nathaniel introduced Tad, and then the father took a bottle out from beneath his cassock. It contained a clear liquid that was obviously of the alcoholic variety and he bustled into the side cabinet next to the desk and brought out six mugs. He poured a generous measure into each one.

'To life and ole friends,' he toasted.

'To life,' agreed everyone.

'Right,' said Axel. 'All be seated, and Nathaniel will tell us his story.'

They sat.

And the Marine told his tale.

CHAPTER 23

The group of reunited friends had stayed up late, finally heading to bed a mere two hours before sunrise to snatch some well needed sleep.

They had also drunk another three bottles of father O'Hara's moonshine and Nathaniel had discovered that, although he might well be immortal, he could still have the mother of all hangovers. As a result, he had arisen later than his usual sunup routine and he had downed a gallon of water, had a cold shower, dressed and then he and Tad headed off to see Axel to wish him goodbye for now.

The two travelers had decided to keep heading towards London and then they hoped to stop in at the abbey once again on the way back home.

When they got to the captain's office he was busy in a meeting, so they sat on a hard wooden bench in the hallway and waited.

As it so happened they didn't have to wait long. After a mere few minutes the door opened, and, to Nathaniel's utter amazement, a short, gray-skinned alien walked out of the office, wished Axel goodbye, and then left, after been escorted by two fully armed battle Orcs.

Axel came to the door and invited them in.

'Sit down, friends,' he said. 'So, are your plans still to leave today?'

Tad was about to reply but Nathaniel butted in. 'What the hell was that?' he asked.

Axel raised an eyebrow. 'What was what?'

'That thing that just walked out of your office.'

'Oh him,' said Axel. That's Pawah Patenemheb, the Fair-Folk ambassador.

Impressive, aren't they? They all look like that.'

'Who's impressive?' asked Nathaniel. 'The pig-faces or the little gray, rubber-skinned bugger?'

Both Tad and Axel looked at the Marine with baffled expressions.

'What gray man?' asked Axel.

Tad stood up and walked over to his friend. 'Nate. Are you okay?'

'Of course I'm okay. What the hell is wrong with you two? What are you talking about?'

'The tall blonde-haired dude that just walked out of the office,' said Tad. 'He's one of the Fair-Folk. I know that you haven't seen one before. They all look remarkably similar. Well built, action men faces, impossible hair.'

Without saying anything Nathaniel jumped up and ran to the window. He could see the gray man flanked by his Orcs walking down the street. He grabbed Axel by the arm and showed him.

'There,' he pointed at the alien. 'That ugly little thing. What is it?'

Both Tad and Axel started to look genuinely worried. 'Umm … that's who we're talking about,' said Axel. 'The Fair-Folk ambassador.'

Nathaniel stared at his friends for almost a full minute. Then he shook his head.

'Good God. You can't see, can you?'

'What?' asked Axel.

'Send someone to get the professor and Father O'Hara,' said Nathaniel. 'We need to talk.'

***

'Well there's no empirical evidence that Nathaniel is correct in what he saw,' said the professor. 'However, given his particular set of skills and the way that he has been affected by the surfeit of gamma radiation in the atmosphere, we can assume that he can see things that we cannot. That leaves us with a couple of questions. Firstly, why does he see a little gray man as opposed to the Aryan-type Adonis that we all see and, secondly, how do the little gray men change our perception of them?'

'Possession,' shouted Father O'Hara. 'The evil sons of bitches have possessed us. We need to carry out an exorcism. Or a cleansing. Sumat like dat,' he continued. 'Actually, to be honest, I'm not dat sure what da church's protocol is regarding little gray men. To be sure dere is naught in da bible about it.'

The father looked grim and sneaked a sip of moonshine from one of his ever-present bottles.

'What worries me,' said Axel. 'Is that they are capable of such mental deceit. If they can make us see what isn't there … well, are they affecting our thinking? And if so, what are they making us think?'

'Look,' said Nathaniel. 'The important thing is that we know. Axel, all of you actually, keep a close eye on any of them when you next meet one. Try to see through their cloak. I assume that it's some sort of mass hypnosis. A mental camouflage of some sort.'

'But why do it?' asked Tad.

'Simple,' replied Axel. 'They have deemed, correctly I add, that we would be more akin to dealing with someone whom we saw as the same as us. As opposed to a foreign alien type. Let's face it—if they looked like Orcs then we would be that much more suspicious but, instead they look like a bunch of male models and that allays our fears. Fears of the unknown, of the strange. The different.'

'Fecking heathens,' grumbled Father O'Hara. 'Dey needs to be drowned in a vat of holy water, dey do. Putting on human faces to fool us. It's immoral. Lying is what it is, and de church don't approve.'

Nathaniel grinned. 'I've missed you, Father. Tell it like it is and hallelujah to the rest.'

'So, what do we do now?' asked Tad

Nathaniel shrugged. 'Not much that

we can do,' he answered. 'Not even sure what difference this all makes. The two of us continue as we were, as does everybody else. We keep our eyes peeled and see what the future brings us.'

'Very fatalistic,' said the professor.

'It's worked for me so far,' said Nathaniel. 'Well, sort of. Tad and I will continue our trip and we'll see you on the return leg. Oh, a favor if you could, Captain? Tad and I have a hundred jars of some sort of fruit preserve that we traded for a couple of days back. Could we trade it for something else? We need to show that we are legitimate traders, no need to blow our cover over something so trivial.'

'We got cigars,' said Father O'Hara. 'Would dose do?'

'Great,' agreed Nathaniel. 'Less weight as well.'

'Drop da preserve off at da chapel before youse go and I'll give you a few cases of cigars. You'll like dem, dey're pretty good.'

Tad and Nathaniel shook hands all

round and left to gather up their horses and baggage. On the way out, they swapped the preserve for cigars and went on their way.

'I wonder if we're up or down on the deals so far?' asked Tad.

'Who cares?' replied Nathaniel. 'It's simply a cover.'

'I care,' said Tad. 'Just because it's a cover doesn't mean that we should do it badly. That offends my sensibilities.'

The Marine laughed, and they rode in silence for a while.

Eventually Tad spoke up again. 'Worked it all out. I reckon that we're well up. Got a good deal on the cigars. Now, as long as we don't smoke them all we could come out of this on top.'

That night they stopped in the woods and set up camp, following Nathaniel's habit of finding a pitch hidden from passersby and well sheltered. They ate a meal of stewed vegetables, drank some uisge and smoked a couple of the cigars.

Neither spoke much. Instead, they simply sat together in a companionable silence that only true friends could find comfortable.

The next morning, they awoke to snow. Light flakes fluttering down and hardly settling. But, by the time they had finished a quick breakfast of bread and cheese, the snow had thickened up enough to coat the trees and ground with a thin white film.

After an hour the snowfall had become a genuine snowstorm and visibility was down to a mere few feet. And then the wind picked up.

Nathaniel and Tad dismounted and started to lead the horses, bending against the wind, desperately looking for some form of shelter.

'I miss weather forecasts,' shouted Nathaniel. 'Even if they were often wrong, at least we had some sort of clue.'

'You're right about that,' answered Tad. 'And I tell you something else, if we don't find shelter soon we aren't going to last through the night. The weather patterns have worsened since you left us and this, in particular, is getting worse by the minute.'

'Hold on,' called Nathaniel. 'This blundering around isn't doing us any good. We could fall off a cliff before we even knew it was there. Stand still, I'm going to try something.'

Nathaniel went down on one knee and then took a deep breath. He blocked out the noise of the howling wind, blanked out the wet flakes of snow, the freezing cold. He relaxed and let his mind flow. He felt the strength of the earth and he cast out his silver net of consciousness, letting it crawl along the ground, under the snow, protected from the storm. Outwards it went. He sensed life, a hare, a fox. Further. Further.

And then, suddenly he was aware of another being. A human. More than an awareness, it was as if they were actually standing next to him. Invisible but palpably there.

'Follow me,' echoed the presence in his head, and the faintest of lights glowed in front of him. This was not at all what the Marine had expected to happen. At best he had thought that he might feel the lie of the land. So, with little choice, he followed.

'Come on, Tad,' he shouted above the keening wind. 'This way.'

The little big man trudged behind him, leading both his horse and the packhorse. Nathaniel broke the path, plowing through the snowdrifts and allowing Tad an easier way.

The Marine followed the glow as it pulsed weakly in front of him, more graveyard-glimmer than leading light. And then suddenly, out of the gloom, two shapes appeared. Men, wrapped in furs, faces covered with woolen balaclavas. They beckoned to Nate and Tad.

Follow,' echoed the voice, as it brushed across the Marine's consciousness like cobwebs on bare skin.

The men guided the two friends through a gap in between two large caravans. They found themselves in a circle of caravans or vardos, as the walking folk called them. Inside the circle, or tabor, the wind immediately lessened. Nathaniel could see that it was because thick sheets of canvas had been tied tight between each of the vardos and between their wheels, forming an almost complete windbreak. As well as this, fully half of the tabor was covered with more canvas and propped up with stout wooden poles. The horses were led to a sheltered area where a group of young boys rubbed them down with straw, gave them hay, and threw blankets over them. Tad and the Marine were led to a central fire under the middle of the covered area.

A large man with a huge moustache stood up and walked over to greet them, his arms flung wide.

'Nathaniel,' he boomed.

The Marine grinned. 'Papa Dante.'

The two men hugged each other, laughing, and clapping each other's backs.

Papa held Nathaniel's shoulders and

looked at him. 'My boy,' he said. 'Gogo told us to expect you, but I still feel as if my eyes deceive my brain. You haven't aged. Over twenty years and you look the same.'

Nathaniel grinned. 'If it's any consolation, Papa, you look pretty good yourself. Not even a gray hair.'

Papa leaned forward and whispered in Nathaniel's ear. 'I dye my hair with henna,' he said. 'An old man's vanity. Our secret.'

Nathaniel stepped back and introduced Tad. Papa shook his hand.

'Come with me,' he said to the Marine. 'Gogo wants to see you. Your friend can sit here.' Papa pointed to one of the piles of fur set around the fire.

A girl came up to Tad and gave him a mug of steaming brew. Nathaniel could smell the alcohol in it from where he stood. The little big man followed the girl to the fire.

Papa led the Marine to one of the vardos and showed him up the stairs.

'I'll be by the fire when you're finished,' he said. 'We shall eat and drink. Tell tall tales and sing songs.' He clapped Nathaniel on the back again. 'It is good to see you after all these years, my friend.'

The Marine opened the door to the vardo and went in.

Gogo was seated at the table, her milky white eyes turned towards him and she smiled. Like Nathaniel, she looked no older than when he had last seen her, some twenty plus years before. She was old then and she was old now.

'Greetings, Forever Man. You look the same.'

'As do you, Gogo,' said Nathaniel. 'But how would you know?'

She laughed. 'I see as well as you, young man,' she said. 'Just not with my eyes. Sit.' She gestured to an empty seat opposite her. There was a mug of some liquid on the table and she pushed it towards the Marine. 'Drink. It will warm you.'

Nathaniel took a sip. It was a brandy.

Rich and golden and sweet. Like a mug full of sunshine. He felt the warmth spread through him.

'It was you who led us here,' he said.

'Of course,' replied Gogo. 'I was waiting for you. 'So, tell me all,' she continued. 'I know the most of it but give me details. They are more important than you know.'

So, once again, the Marine told his saga.

CHAPTER 24

The storm raged on and, after Nathaniel had told his story to Gogo he was obliged to tell it yet again to Papa Dante and his people. By then he was thoroughly sick of talking about himself and it was a great pleasure to simply sit back, drink in hand, and listen to the great raconteur that was Papa Dante.

The bad weather continued and for the next two days he spent most of his spare moments with Gogo who was helping him to hone his mental magik techniques.

Firstly, she asked him to draw in some power, just enough to light a flame. While he did this, she laid her hands on his head and concentrated.

'Aha,' she proclaimed. 'I thought so. Very clever. I see that you envisage your consciousness as a silver threaded net, cast out across the countryside to reel in your power. As I said, clever, but inefficient. You see, nets can be broken. Cut. They have holes in through which stuff can escape. Instead of the net, I want you to imagine your consciousness as a sheet of light. And not just any light. The same light that you see in the skies every day. The pulse light. The same colors, the way that it moves, pulsing and coruscating. Like it's alive.'

Nathaniel tried. And it proved to be more difficult than holding on to a greased hog. But, slowly, after a few more hours, he had it under control, spreading the light out all around him. Enveloping the landscape in his mental radiance.

'Good,' encouraged Gogo. 'Bring it back in. Remember to pull the power back with it.'

The Marine drew the light back to him. He could feel it throbbing with earth-power. Sparking and surging.

'Now,' said Gogo, 'a small flame.'

Nathaniel opened his hand, palm up, and imagined a small ball of fire floating above it. There was a rush of air and a burning globe appeared in front of him. Spitting and crackling with power, white-hot, like a miniature sun. The interior of the vardo heated up instantly as the ball of raging energy pumped out waves of heat.

'Turn it off,' commanded Gogo. 'Quickly!'

Nathaniel shut his mind down. Imagining black cold emptiness. The ball of pure energy spluttered out of existence. All that was left was the residue of heat and a blue-white spot that seemed to be branded into the Marine's retina.

'Impressive,' admitted Gogo. 'Your control needs a bit of working on, but I think that you get the gist of it.' She smiled and grasped Nathaniel's hand. 'Well done, Forever Man. Now, keep working on it. Not only fire but also ice, water, wind. Now go. Relax by the fire, listen to more of Papa Dante's ridiculous stories, eat and drink. The weather has almost broken and, I think, you will leave us tomorrow. I bid you goodbye. But we shall meet again—sooner than you think.'

The Marine kissed her on both cheeks and left her vardo to spend the rest of his time amongst the walking folk.

***

They left early the next morning after trading some cigars for some of the golden brandy that the walking folk made so well.

The sky shimmered with the rainbow colors of the pulse and the drifts of pure diamond-white snow reflected it back in an exhilarating show of prismatic light. It was like riding through an artist's fantasy. A stained-glass window of a world.

The horses' hooves crunched through the snow and their breath plumed out in front of them. Both Nate and Tad had broken out their furs and pulled them tightly around themselves to ward off the bitter cold.

Nathaniel contemplated using his

newfound power to encase them both in a pocket of warm air but decided against it, lest he lose control and ended up crispy-frying both of them instead.

They followed the old M1 highway through the country, heading towards London. Although it had been over twenty years since the pulse, the highway was still full of derelict cars. Rusting reminders of a bygone era where the trip that they were taking would have been a mere five- or six-hour jaunt—as opposed to many days of hard walking and horseback travel.

Late afternoon they would divert from the remains of the highway and seek a village or town where they would trade a little, eat a hot meal, and barter for a room.

Some of the smaller villages were doing fairly well, albeit under the ever-present yoke of either the Fair-Folk or their worthy humans.

The norm seemed to be that every settlement of more than a hundred people had a detachment of Fair-Folk control attached to it. Some small villages had only a small battle group living amongst them. Ten Orcs and five goblins with a human cavalry messenger and at least one worthy human.

Bigger towns, such as St. Ipolytes or Gosmoor, had a thousand or so humans and full detachments of battle Orcs and goblins complete with an actual Fair-Folk ambassador.

Tad and Nathaniel came across another two more Fair-Folk but, try as he might, Tad could only see them as six foot, impossibly perfect, androgynous male-model types, whereas Nathaniel saw the reality of the situation.

But one thing that they both noticed was the social structure that had been imposed on the survivors of the human race. Humanity had been relegated to the role of the ground-grubbing serf. Any less menial labor, such as blacksmithing, trade, or administration could only be done by those who had been accepted as a worthy human or else had obtained a certificate of permission through some other means, usually bribery of a worthy human. All crimes, no matter how petty, invoked capital punishment and all executions were carried out in public, by the rope.

Man had truly returned to the dark ages and this filled Nathaniel with righteous ire.

After spending the night in the town of Findon, another sewage-ridden, gray, depressing survival camp of a place, Nathaniel made a decision.

'Let's go home,' he said to Tad. 'I see no reason to continue to London. I have seen enough.'

'Are you sure?'

The Marine nodded. 'The world stinks. Literally and figuratively. It's worse than Russia at the height of its madness. I'm not sure what can be done, but I'll tell you something for nothing, something will be done. I need to think about it. We'll head home via the abbey. And I think that this time I'll talk to Milly, whatever the reaction.'

They trudged back through the snow, traveling a slightly different route to the way that they had just come. They were stopped once by an Orc battle group and questioned by a worthy human who demanded to see their papers. He had also demanded a box of cigars and two flagons of brandy as "tax." The Orcs and goblins had merely stared at them without expression, their weapons at the ready.

A few days later they arrived back at the abbey and called on Axel.

Nathaniel asked the captain to send for the professor and the father, so that they could talk.

When all were seated he began.

'My friends. When I left this timeline, some twenty years back, humanity was in crises. The ongoing solar flares had all but destroyed us, driving us back into a pre-agrarian economy. A society of hunters, gatherers, and scavengers. As you know, we died in our millions. And then the so-called Fair-Folk with their pig-men and their goblins took over and, in doing so, forced humanity forward into a true agrarian age. An age of crop producers.

Dirt farmers, toiling the soil to make ends meet. Many seem to think that this is what saved humanity. Bullcrap! Double bullcrap,' the Marine banged his fist on the table.

'Estimates show that, at the end of the first year there were no more than five, maybe six million people left. Say six million. Living on over three hundred million acres of land. That gives us over fifty acres each. We would have survived. Okay, there was a bandit problem, but that too would have passed as we banded together. What I am saying is that we owe these Fair-Folk nothing. In fact, they have done us, as humans, irreparable harm. Humanity has been subjugated. We have been chained to the soil. The only way to get a little ahead is to become a party member. To repudiate your own race. And then all that you have done is raise yourself from dirt-grubber to ass-licker.'

The Marine stopped and lit himself a cigar, using his magik to create a small flame to do so. It wasn't necessary, as he could have easily used a taper from the fire, but he felt that he needed a little showmanship. He let the flame burn in the air in front of him for a while before flicking it out of existence.

'Friends, I cannot allow this to continue. Mankind was not meant to be enslaved to a group of gray aliens and pig-faced monsters. However, there is no way that we can fight against them. Not yet. They are too many and too well trained and armed. What I propose is this. I will return to Scotland. There I will, once again, unite the clans. I will fortify and protect Hadrian's Wall and I shall declare the land north of the wall a free state. No Fair-Folk shall be allowed there under pain of death. Any human that wants to live a life free from the yolk of the gray things will be welcome to the Scottish Free State. There they will be protected, and they will be able to pursue whatever they will, as long as they follow the rules of the state.'

'And who shall rule this land?' asked the professor.

'I shall,' said Nathaniel. 'As well as a council of advisors that I appoint.'

'You'll be like a king of old,' commented the prof.

Nathaniel shook his head. 'No, I shall not be like a king of old. I will be a king of old. King Nathaniel Degeo Arnthor Hogan, the first of his line.'

'Not to put too fine a point on it, my boy,' argued the prof. 'But what gives you the right?'

Nathaniel smiled, but there was no humor in his expression.

'I claim the right, professor. As the only immortal amongst us I claim the right. As a conqueror of the Romans I claim the right. As the last king of the Picts … I claim the right. And any that gainsay me will be face my wrath. For is it not said—don't screw with The Forever Man?'

'Works for me,' said Axel. 'How can we help?'

'By creating a pipeline,' said Nathaniel. 'Once we bloody the Fair-Folk's noses and make plain our plans, they will not stand idly by. At very least they will ban any humans from leaving their realm and going over to the free state. I want you and the church to set up a pipeline whereby we can smuggle people out of the realm and into my kingdom.'

'It shall be done,' said Axel.

Father O'Hara nodded his agreement. 'I too am wid you, Nathaniel.'

'I too,' agreed the prof.

'As ever, my friend,' added Tad. 'As ever.'

The four of them stayed up late into the night. Throwing out ideas and laying down plans.

The next morning, when Tad and Nathaniel left, the seed of the Free State of Scotland had been planted, it had germinated and was ready to grow.

CHAPTER 25

Milly was exhausted. It seemed that the bulk of her job was to fill in paperwork, and the mere sight of the gray, lumpy recycled board that passed for paper in the new world made her feel ill just to look at.

There were licenses to trade, to work metal, to buy, to sell. Permits to allow extra food for pregnant women, travel permits, and living permits.

There were countless applications from people for extra housing, food, clothing. Applications for people applying to become worthy humans. Petitions, letters of advice, and even some of complaint—although those were guarded and couched in such a way as to make them almost impossible to understand. After all, dissent was a capital punishment.

The applications to become worthy humans were simply discarded immediately. The Fair-Folk had decided that the quota for worthies had been met and, for the foreseeable future, no more humans would be elevated.

She also had two hangings to preside over later that week. One was for domestic violence, a husband beating his wife, and the other was a teenage boy who had been caught stealing seed grain and bartering it on the black market.

She knew that some still viewed capital punishment as harsh, but she well remembered the times before the Fair-Folk and their laws. Barely staying alive on a diet of leathery old potatoes, living in constant fear of bandit raids. Then being kidnapped and viciously violated. Repeatedly. And it didn't end there. Still, almost twenty years on, she relived the experience almost nightly. The stink of their breath, the tearing pain. The feeling of utter helplessness as a line of men queued up to take their turn at despoiling you. Over and over and over.

A few hangings were a small price to pay to prevent the same happening to any other young girls. The Fair-Folk had their problems but at least they weren't animals … like her fellow human beings.

There was a knock on the door. Her assistant, Doris Finburg. Late middle age, efficient, timid. An apology of a person, not a worthy, but striving to do her best.

'Ma'am,' she said, her voice a little above a whisper as it always was. 'A gentleman to see you. He doesn't have an appointment, but he says that it's urgent. He says that he has come to apologize.'

Normally Milly saw no one without prior appointment, however, this piqued her interest. Apologize? About what, she wondered.

'Show him in, Doris.'

Her assistant ushered a man in and then closed the door.

He was tall. Well built. His dark hair tumbled in waves past his shoulders and his neatly trimmed beard framed a strong jaw and straight nose. His eyes were an almost ethereal green. And they bored right into her very soul.

She gasped, and her hand flew to her heart. She struggled to breathe, and it felt as if someone had placed a huge boulder on her chest and left her to die.

'Hello, Milly,' he said.

Finally, she managed to draw a breath and she stepped around the desk on wobbly legs. She walked right up to him, curled her right hand into a fist and struck him in the face as hard as she could.

The Marine could have dodged but he didn't. He stood stock-still and took the blow. A cut opened up above his left eye and blood flowed down his face. Milly pulled her arm back and struck him again, this time splitting his lip. The third punch, however, slapped into the Marine's palm and he held her fist tight.

'Let me go,' she grunted. 'Afraid that I'll hurt you?'

Nathaniel shook his head. 'No. I'm afraid that you might hurt yourself.'

The two of them stared at each other for a while. Eventually Milly spoke.

'You left me,' she said. 'You left me, and then the bad men came, and they took me, and they hurt me. And you weren't there.'

'I'm sorry, Milly,' said Nathaniel. 'I am so sorry.'

'I hate you,' hissed Milly.

'I'm sorry.'

Milly kicked the Marine in the shins. Hard. He didn't flinch.

'I hate you so much,' Milly cried out.

She threw her arms around him; tears flowing freely from her eyes as her body shook with emotion.

'I thought you were dead,' she said. 'Every day for twenty years I have lived with your death and now you've come back.'

She held him as hard as she could.

'I hate you,' she whispered into his chest. Nathaniel stroked her hair and said nothing. She looked up at him.

They kissed.

CHAPTER 26

The two of them had departed the collective at a gallop and had ridden the horses hard, steaming and panting through the frozen landscape.

That night they camped in a secluded dell, a way off the beaten track. Due to the haste of their travel that day, they had little time to talk.

'I still don't understand why we had to run,' said Tad. 'You wouldn't sleep with her, so she said that she would send the Orcs to hunt you down and kill you?'

Nathaniel nodded. 'Basically. It was a bit more complicated than that, but, in a nutshell—yes.'

'Wow,' exclaimed Tad. 'That is seriously heavy.'

'The whole thing was pretty heavy,

man,' said Nathaniel. 'First thing she hits me, says that she hates me, and then we kiss. Then I tell her that I need some time to assimilate. I mean … a year ago, to me, she was a little girl. So, she screams that I'm rejecting her again, I try and calm her down. She asks me to stay and I tell her that I need to go back to Scotland. I explained the whole plan to her, begged her to come back with me, but by now she's totally lost her cool. Screaming and shouting that I'm deserting her again, tells me that I'm a traitor and a usurper. Says that I'm worse than an animal. And then she threatens me with Orcs. I figured that we'd better get going while the going was still good.'

'Women, hey?' Sighed Tad.

Nathaniel poked at the fire with a stick. 'Yeah, women.' He looked around him, surveying the land. 'Hey, you know, back when, before I met you, I rescued some guy here. In this approximate area. He was naked. Bit of a loony, actually. So, I found out that he had escaped from this lunatic asylum, or home for the mentally challenged or whatever they called it back then. I found the place and returned him. Stayed the night. Next morning, I went to find him to say goodbye … the guy's dead. Strung up in a butcher's room, sliced and bloody diced. Waiting to be eaten by the staff there. Then I realize that the meal I ate the night before had been people flesh. I tell you, Tad, sometimes life is simply too weird to contemplate.'

'What did it taste like?'

'Pork,' said Nathaniel. 'Fatty pork.'

'Did you kill the cannibals?'

The Marine shook his head. 'No. They were keeping the loonies alive. If I killed them then everyone would have died.'

'They were going to die anyway,' said Tad. 'They were going to be eaten.'

'I know. But I left them. I didn't know what to do then and I don't know what to do now.'

'There's nothing that you can do about Milly,' said Tad. 'It's simply too complicated. Tell you what. Why don't we get you home and organize you a nice uncomplicated war to fight? You like that don't you?'

Nathaniel laughed. 'You sarcastic little bastard.'

Tad offered the Marine a cigar and they sat smoking until it was time to turn in.

***

The first thing that they noticed when they rode over the hill was the gallows.

It stood out starkly against the rising sun. Its single arm stretching out to the side, holding a thirteen-knot noose of death. An implacable inanimate object that's sole purpose was to choke the life out of a human being.

The sight of it brought on a cold rage in Nathaniel's soul.

'Look,' he pointed. 'I hate those things. Some poor bastard is going to hang for stealing a loaf of bread, or selling food without permission, or for working without a permit.'

'Or maybe for murder or rape,' said Tad. 'We don't know.'

The Marine kicked his horse into a trot, urging it forward.

'Well, let's go and find out,' he said.

It was a small village and the gallows were set up on the fringe, in the middle of an open patch of ground. This allowed standing room for the crowd who would be watching, whether they wanted to or not.

The two friends headed towards the middle of the village, seeking the pub and some information about the forthcoming hanging. Nathaniel stopped a young boy who was walking down the street.

'Hey,' he called. 'Boy. Where's the inn.'

The child pointed at a building and then ran.

'You have a real way with children,' said Tad, laughing as he did so.

The Marine growled. 'Sod it.'

They hitched their horses to the rail outside the inn and went in. Tad brought a box of cigars to barter.

Nathaniel sat down at a table and Tad chatted to the barman for a while and then traded a handful of cigars for a small bottle of some type of white spirit flavored with plums. He sat down opposite the Marine, put two mugs down on the table, filled them and placed the bottle in the middle, easy for both to reach.

Nate took a slug of the liquor. It tasted like paint thinners with slight overtones of rotten fruit. He poured another, lit a cigar, and sat back in his chair.

'Barman says that the lucky person getting his neck stretched is some old dude. Says that he's a mental case.'

'What's he getting hung for?' asked Nate.

'Equivocation,' said Tad.

'What?'

'Equivocation. You know, deception, misrepresentation.'

'Talking crap?'

Tad nodded. 'Basically. Yep, equivocation is basically talking crap.'

The Marine shook his head. 'There is no way that someone is going to be hung to death for bullshitting. Not on my watch. Anyway, what did he talk crap about?'

Tad shook his head. 'The barman's not too sure about that. Seems to think that he's a harmless old nutter that simply overstepped the mark.'

The Marine looked around at the other people in the bar room. A group of young men. Two sets of middle-aged couples. A trio of old farming types and a couple of lone drinkers.

'Look at them,' he said to Tad, a look of utter disdain on his face. 'An old man is going to be hung for less than no reason and they do nothing.'

Tad shrugged. 'Not all people are hardwired the way that you are, Nate. They see a windmill and assume that it's a device for grinding corn or whatever. You see one and it's all, grab your lance and charge the bugger. If these people rebel, the Orcs will chop them into little itty-bitty human kebobs. So, they look the other way, they convince themselves that it's the right thing to do. They live lives of constant low-level fear, of quiet desperation. After all, they're only human.'

The Marine spat on the floor. 'They are beneath contempt,' he growled.

The barman looked up and was about to say something when he saw the look on Nathaniel's face. He hurriedly looked down and busied himself polishing his counter top.

The Marine stood up. 'Hey, barkeep. Where is this old dude being kept?'

'We don't have a jail, sir,' answered the barman. 'He's in the shop opposite. In the basement. Worthy human Johnson and Orc Sergeant Dob are guarding him.'

'Where is the rest of the battle group?' asked Nathaniel.

The barman hesitated. It was obvious that he wanted to enquire as to why

Nathaniel was so interested in the Orc battle groups whereabouts, but a stern look from the Marine put a halt to his curiosity.

'At the end of the main street, sir,' he continued. 'Small camp. Another eight Orcs and five goblins.'

The Marine tossed back the last of his drink and beckoned to Tad.

'Let's go, grab a bottle of uisge and another box of cigars.'

Tad followed Nate across the street, pausing to fetch the merchandise that the Marine had asked for.

They opened the door to the general store and walked in. The shop was piled high with goods, most of them dusty and obviously worth little. Rusted shovels, badly cobbled boots, a selection of leathery old root vegetables. A cracked oil lamp.

A shop keeper sat on a bar stool behind the counter and another male sat in the corner, reading an ancient, yellowed old copy of Harry Potter. Its cover was torn and faded, and it was showing every one of its eighty years of wear and tear.

Nathaniel assumed that the second male was the worthy human Johnson and walked over to him.

'Hi, we'd like to talk to the prisoner.'

The worthy human didn't even bother to look up from his tale of teenage wizardry, he simply shook his head. 'No.'

Nate flicked his fingers at Tad who handed over the uisge and the cigars. The Marine thrust them under the worthy's face, pushing his book aside.

'Here is a bribe,' he said, his voice dripping with contempt.

The worthy opened the box of cigars and smelled it. Then he did the same with the uisge. He nodded. 'Downstairs. Tell the Orc I said that you could see the prisoner. Tell him that you're a priest or something.'

The two of them tramped down the stairs into the cellar. There was a small storage area at the foot of the staircase. An Orc sat on a stool in the middle of the area, behind him a door with a barred cut-out in the middle.

'We're here to see the prisoner,' said Nathaniel. 'We're priests. The worthy said that we could.'

The Orc stared at the two men. Nathaniel couldn't gauge what it was thinking. Its deep-set eyes, and lack of nose made it impossible to impart human expression. For all the Marine knew, it was as pissed off as all hell, or maybe ecstatically happy. However, knowing the military bent of mind, Nathaniel assumed, quite rightly as it was, that the Orc was simply bored. He took out a set of keys and unlocked the door.

'Go in,' he commanded.

The two of them went into the small cellar room and the Orc locked the door behind them.

The old man looked up at the two of them with unveiled curiosity, he looked to be in his early seventies, a salt-and-pepper beard, slightly balding, but well-built and a good posture. He stood up and took a step towards them, grimacing slightly as he did so. Then he stuck his hand out in greeting.

'G'day, strangers,' he said. 'Name's Mahoney. Brian Mahoney, but my mates call me Roo, as in kangaroo. So, priests you say? Well, forgive me for not believing but I'll be a monkey's bum before I see either of you wearing the cloth, if you don't mind.'

Nathaniel smiled. 'Australian?' he asked.

'Born and bred, me old mukka,' confirmed the old man as he rubbed his knee with his hands. 'Bloody arthritis,' he mumbled. 'Curse of ageing, I suppose. Anyhow, I was a mechanical engineer back in the day. Came out to limey-land some twenty-five years ago on holiday, pulse struck, and I was stranded here. No bloody sun, no good rum, and the Sheilas all have funny accents. Now I'm in jail, only a day away from being executed for bugger-knows-what. I'll tell you something for nothing, maties, this is the last time I come to bloody England for my hols.'

'So, what are you in for?' asked Tad.

'Well, official charge is equivocation. Can you believe it? But that's all bullshine it is. They banged me up because they were scared that I was telling the truth.'

'About what?'

The old man leant in close and dropped his voice to a whisper.

'You know the Fair-Folk?'

Tad nodded. 'Seen a few of them. Tall, blonde. Bunch of male models.'

'Bullshine,' whispered Roo. 'Bull and shine. They're not a bunch of tall blonde woofters at all. They're actually a bunch of short little gray buggers with big heads and skin like a dolphin. Ugly little beggars to say the least.'

'You can see that?' asked Nathaniel.

'Well, yes,' confirmed Roo. 'And no.'

'What do you mean,' insisted Nathaniel. 'Is it yes or no?'

'Both,' continued the old man. 'If I look directly at them they look like a bunch competing for Britain's top model. But if you see them reflected in a mirror or a window … hey presto, little gray men.'

'Really?' questioned Tad. 'How come everybody else doesn't see that?'

Roo shrugged. 'Don't know. Maybe some do. Maybe no one else has seen them in front of a reflective surface. Whatever, they don't want me spreading the news so it's the drop for poor old Brian Mahoney. Don't actually know why—it's not as if anyone believes me.'

'We believe you,' said Nathaniel. 'I know, because I can see them as they are. Even without the reflection thing. Little aliens with gray skin and big eyes.'

Roo's face lit up with a huge smile. 'Well that's great,' he said. 'At least I can die knowing that I'm not actually a complete nutter.' He stared at Nate for a while. 'Unless, of course, you're also a nutjob.'

The Marine shook his head. 'Might be, but not when it comes to the aliens. Look, Roo, I'm not going to let them hang you. We're busting you out of here. You game?'

'Bloody right, I'm game,' assured Roo. 'When?'

'Now,' replied the Marine.

'How are you going to incapacitate the Orc?' asked Tad.

'Permanently,' answered Nathaniel.

'Bit harsh, he's only doing his job.'

'Yeah,' agreed the Marine. 'So were all the dudes that worked for Hitler. You ready?'

Tad and Roo nodded.

'Hey, Orc,' yelled Nathaniel. 'We've done our priest stuff. Let us out.'

The Orc shuffled over to the door, unlocked it, and swung it open. Instead of drawing his axe, Nathaniel took note of what Tad had said about being over-harsh and so he swung a huge roundhouse punch at the Orc instead. The massive blow struck the creature a perfect shot on its temple.

The Orc flinched slightly and looked at the Marine with a puzzled expression on its flat face.

'What's that in aid of?' it asked.

Nathaniel struck again. This time putting the full weight of his body behind the blow. He aimed at the Orc's chest and the punch landed with a sound like an axe chopping into an oak tree.

He managed to knock the creature back a whole step.

Then the Orc punched him back.

The blow lifted the Marine off his feet and slammed him against the wall. The sound of his ribs breaking could be heard clearly above the meaty smack of the Orc's fist landing.

Nathaniel slid down the wall to the floor, his vision a mess of dark and light. Then he shook his head and stood back up. Tad kicked the Orc behind his right knee causing the creature to turn and face him.

'Hey, Nate,' he shouted. 'You'd better do something quick, before this monster pops my head like a pimple.'

Nathaniel breathed in deeply. Ignoring the pain from his broken ribs, he cast out an orb of light and then drew the power back in. Then he struck the Orc again, his fist thundering into the side of the thing's face.

Its eyes rolled back into its head, leaving only the whites showing, and it sank slowly to the floor.

'Mother of God,' grunted Nathaniel. 'Those buggers are tough. Next time, no more mister nice guy. Any more of them gets some axe-time. End of story. Come on, guys.'

The Marine led the way up the stairs and into the shop.

The worthy human jumped up from his seat. 'You can't take the prisoner,' he shouted. 'It's forbidden.'

Nathaniel backhanded him without even slowing his pace. The casual blow smashed the worthy's nose flat and snapped off his two front teeth. 'Forbid that, dickhead.'

The shopkeeper held both his hands up. 'No arguments here,' he said.

Tad picked up the box of cigars and the bottle of uisge as he walked past the downed worthy.

The three men jogged to the horses, Roo lagging slightly behind as he favored the limp in his right leg.

They mounted up, Roo riding the packhorse, and then cantered out of the village, heading in the opposite direction to the Orc battle group.

CHAPTER 27

'Theater,' said Roo.

'What?' asked the Marine.

'You've got to give the punters a bit of theater, mate,' answered Roo. 'Back in 2018 I ran for mayor of Woomalong, southeast Australia, learned a thing or two about politics. And I'm telling you, mate— theater. Give the blokes a show. You can't just go bashing into a fellow's house and tell him that you're the new leader of the clans and you're going to create a new free state for humans and he's got to join you. That simply won't work.'

'Well, obviously,' agreed Nathaniel.

'So then, what's your plan?' asked Roo.

'I figured that we'd start with Tad's friends. He's got nine that are fully committed to the idea. They're a good bunch, tough, hard, good in a fight. Then we'd go from village to village and drum up support. I've done it before.'

'Yep, I know,' said Roo. 'But before, you told me that you challenged the ruling chiefs to mortal combat every time.'

'That's true,' agreed Nate.

'That's not gonna make you any friends in this day and age, mate. You gotta convince them to follow you because they want to. Okay, I'm not saying that a bit of mortal combat won't be needed, after all, these are violent times. I simply figured that there must be an easier way to go about it.'

'What do you suggest then, Roo?' asked the Marine.

'I've got the beginnings of an idea,' said the Australian. 'Firstly, I need to meet with these nine mates of Tad's. Spend a little time with them. Then I need about two weeks to carry out my plan.'

'Seems reasonable,' said Nate. 'What is the plan?'

Roo shook his head. 'Surprise. Have some trust in the old man, I've been around the block a few times and I know what I'm talking about. Remember, I owe you my life, Chief, I won't let you down.'

The Marine smiled his agreement.

***

The two weeks had turned into just over three and Nathaniel was champing at the bit with impatience. But Tad had convinced him to wait for Roo to complete his task.

The Marine spent the bulk of his time concentrating on his magiks and by the end of the third week he could conjure up and control fireballs about the size of a bowling ball. As well as bring them into existence, he could now actually fire them and hit a man-sized target at over two hundred yards. Conjuring up balls of ice was proving to be a little more difficult and, as for wind, he simply couldn't even get the tiniest of zephyrs blowing. But, all in all, he was happy with his progress and, as Tad had said, the fireballs were super-darn impressive.

Now was the morning of Roo's big reveal and the old Australian engineer was seriously excited.

He called Nathaniel into the sitting room. There was a bulky object standing on the table in the middle of the room, covered with a blanket so that Nate couldn't see what it was.

Roo was rubbing his hands.

'Where's Tad?' asked the Marine.

'Outside, around the back,' answered Roo. 'That's not important right now. So, Chief, without further ado.'

The Aussie ripped the blanket off the table.

Lying on the wooden top was a suit of lightweight armor. A breast and back plate, shoulder guards, vambraces for the arms, greaves for the legs, and a leather kilt reinforced with thin steel plates. Next to the suit was a pair of cunningly crafted gauntlets, as well as a pair of steel-covered combat boots.

The armor itself was a deep blue-black except for a silver infinity logo on the front of the breastplate.

'Come on,' said Roo. 'Try it on, I'll help you.'

The engineer handed Nathaniel a long linen tunic and the Marine disrobed and put the tunic on. Then came the armor.

It fitted perfectly.

'Roo, this is amazing,' said Nathaniel as he clipped his axe onto the belt. 'How did you do it?'

'Car parts, doors, sheet metal. Reinforced by lamination. I worked in a tractor factory back in the day. Made prototypes, so I was well used to working with this type of stuff. It's light but it'll stop any sword. Maybe even an axe. I had help, everyone pitched in, and that's not all. Come on.'

Roo led the Marine through to the back door and ushered him outside.

Standing in the yard, in two lines of five, were Tad and his nine friends. All were dressed in similar armor except for the fact that theirs was a deep blood-red. They also had the infinity symbol etched in silver across the front of their chest plates.

As Nathaniel stepped out of the small cottage, the ten men drew their swords as one and thrust them into the air.

'Forever Man. Oorah!' they shouted in unison.

And behind them a black banner with a silver eternity symbol embroidered on it, unfurled in the Scottish wind, cracking, and snapping at the top of the lance that it was tied to.

Roo smiled hugely. 'Theater,' he said.

CHAPTER 28

For two months they trained. The Forever Man and The Ten.

On horseback with sword and lance. Throwing the javelin from horseback. Attacking on foot. They ran, they pushed weights and then they ran some more. They also spent a lot of time mastering a weapon that Roo had copied from the Australian Aborigines, the woomera. This was basically a three-foot-long piece of wood with a groove cut into it and a small cup at the one end. The woomera was used to launch a heavy arrow-like missile. The added length and leverage allowing the thrower to propel a four-foot long missile over one hundred yards with great accuracy. Nathaniel agreed with Roo that this would negate the need for archers.

The Marine pushed them like they

were raw recruits back at Parris Island Marine basics camp.

'It's not enough to look good,' he told them. 'We also have to be good. You have to be the best because, from here on out, you will be known across the land as The Ten.'

At the end of the two months The Ten were a lean, mean fighting machine.

Nathaniel was ready to go canvassing.

They started at the nearby village of Drumcroy. There was no campaigning plan as such, they simply mounted up and rode into the village early in the morning, halting in front of the main inn or on the village square. Then they would simply stand there. It wouldn't be long and one of the village seniors would pitch up and ask what they were doing.

Nathaniel would give them a short version of their mission to create a free human state and then he would request a town meeting for that evening.

After that, Marine would retire, taking a room at the inn or wherever available, so as to retain his mystique and The Ten would circulate amongst the townsfolk. His men would tell the Marine's story. They would encourage people to consult the old books to look for paintings or images of King Arthur, they would swear to the honesty of the tale. And, by that evening, the villagers would at very least be keen to see what this was all about, and, at most, they would already be true believers.

When all had gathered around, Nathaniel would tell them his vision. He would talk about the Fair-Folk and how they were subjugating the human race. He would tell of the laws and the hangings. He would regale them with tales of how humanity was being strangled, how they would never progress under the yoke of the aliens.

And then he would tell them about the Free State of Scotland. A land where humans could be free, and the pig-face men and their alien masters were not allowed.

Then he would magik up a fireball and

blast it into the heavens. As it exploded high above them he would shout out, asking for volunteers to join his army.

Many hands always shot up.

Because Roo had been correct—theater worked.

Dewar, Pensfold, Croftgarden, and more. Village after town after village. The days became weeks and the weeks became months.

Nathaniel barely slept.

All volunteers would follow Nathaniel and The Ten as they visited village after village, and when the Marine had one thousand followers he would send them to the Wardrew Woods on the river Irthing. It was here that Roo and a team of younger men with building skills had taken the first volunteers and built a military camp based on a batch of drawings that Nathaniel had drawn up for him. "Camp Infinity." The older man's energy seemed to be unflagging and he had become an essential cog in the Marine's burgeoning new machine. His vast intelligence and experience were invaluable.

Next to the river and close to both Hadrian's Wall with plentiful oak for building, it was the perfect spot. Firstly, the engineer had taken care of living quarters, rows and rows of dwellings that were a combination of thatch and oiled cloth, latrines, ablution areas, and covered eating areas. Then he constructed lunging rings for the horses, paddocks, stables, and arenas. Javelin ranges for both spear and woomera and a huge flat parade ground area for drilling and marching.

He had also erected a range of huge workshops that churned out simple armor converted from the thousands of cars that were still scattered throughout the old road systems. Every man got a breastplate, arm guards, and greaves as well as a shield, a hand-and-a-half broadsword, a dagger, a fighting hatchet—similar to a tomahawk—a woomera with arrows, and a javelin.

Men who arrived with a horse went straight into the cavalry where they were issued with similar equipment apart from the sword, which was a curved cavalry saber. Any firearms and ammunition were appropriated and locked up in the camp strong room. However, there was not that much. The United Kingdom had never had much of a gun culture and by now, over twenty years on from the pulse, most ammunition had been used up on either hunting or self-defense. But, whatever there was became the property of The Forever Man.

After discussion with Nathaniel, they had created a simple rank and command structure for the army.

When each thousand men arrived, they were told to vote amongst themselves to choose a captain as a group leader and four sergeants to assist him. When this had been done, the thousand would be broken into four groups of two hundred and fifty, one for each sergeant. The sergeants would then choose five corporals to assist each of them. Each corporal would be put in charge of fifty men. The system was quick and simple, and it worked well.

The cavalry worked under the same strictures except the groups were smaller, only two hundred and fifty so, as always happens with mounted units, there was a much higher officer ratio.

Nathaniel had given each of The Ten, bar Tad, the rank of colonel. Then he had given both Roo and Tad the rank of general. Tad simply shook his head when told and "forgot" to ever put his rank insignia on and Roo had simply told him to 'bugger off,' as he didn't have time for that sort of crap and anyway, he thought that all officers were woofters.

The Forever Man could not have asked for a better team.

***

Six months on and it had been two whole months since the last of Nathaniel's ten thousand strong army had arrived at Camp Infinity.

Under Nathaniel's orders, Roo and a group of ex-architects had spent the last two weeks traveling the length of

Hadrian's Wall, mapping out a repair schedule for it. There was no way that they could restore the entire structure with dressed stone, so they had decided on wooden log retaining walls filled with a mortar made of mud, gravel, and cow dung. The team had repaired and rebuilt a small section to show Nathaniel and the Marine was impressed.

Now all that remained was to do the same for the entire length of the wall. At the same time, they had decided to stick to the original Roman design in having a fort laced every mile, large enough to garrison seventy-five men. Every tenth milefort would be a larger version that would garrison five hundred men so that no minor fort was further than five miles away from major reinforcements. There would also be four full detachments of cavalry, each consisting of two hundred and fifty men, patrolling the wall on the Fair-Folk side, ranging out and scouting to bring back a constant flow of information and intelligence.

It was during one of the nightly

meetings that were held between the three of them, Nathaniel, Roo, and the little big man, that Tad brought up the necessity for taxes.

'Look, Nate,' he said. 'This is all well and good and, militarily I can't fault you, but very soon we are going to run out of food. Already we have to range ten miles or more for game and the stocks of food that the men all brought with them are dangerously low.'

'So, what do you suggest?' the Marine had asked.

'We need to put together teams of mounted tax collectors. Ten men and a couple of wagons would suffice. Maybe ten teams to start with. I'll handpick the leaders, men with a bit of sense. They range far and wide and collect food. Nothing too onerous, just a little from everyone so that we can support our standing army.'

'Tad also had another idea,' interjected Roo. 'He reckons that they should attempt to collect precious metals.

Gold, silver, and copper if they can. Not a lot. A ring or two, a necklace, charm bracelet from each household.'

'Why?' asked Nathaniel.

'Well, Chief,' continued the old Aussie. 'The two of us have concocted a grand plan, we're both still not one hundred percent convinced that it'll work so, as always, we'll reveal all when I think that it's finished and working.'

'Okay,' agreed The Forever Man. 'But what if they don't want to contribute. By my own promises, this is a free area, I can't force them.'

There was an uncomfortable silence for a while. Eventually Tad spoke. 'Freedom comes with a price,' he said. 'I'll tell the boys that contribution isn't obligatory, but it is … advisable.'

'I don't like that,' said Nathaniel.

'Well, you'll like it a lot less when your army all goes home so that they can get a bite to eat. Wake up, Nate. You've been a king before. Where did you think all the revenue came from? The people gotta give and that's that. Sometimes the only way to be truly free is to voluntarily give up some of that freedom.'

As it happened Nathaniel had no need to worry. The people gave willingly and, those that genuinely couldn't were either let off or, in some cases, Nathaniel's men actually gave them food from out of the tax wagons.

Gold and silver were a little harder to come by but, after a month of collecting, a surprisingly large amount of bullion was stashed in the camp strong room under lock and key as well as armed guard.

By now Nathaniel had set thousands of men to rebuilding the wall and it was going along at a rate that far exceeded the speed anything the Romans had achieved so many thousands of years before.

***

It was a clear day. The solar flares pulsed across the heavens, rainbow colors rippling across the skies in scintillating waves. A light breeze snapped and pulled at the black and silver banner of The Forever Man and visibility was clean and sharp.

Nathaniel saw them coming from over five miles away. Marching in fifteen columns of five. Seventy-five of them. Fifty battle Orcs and twenty-five goblin archers.

On each side of the Marine, teams of soldiers worked the dirt. Mixing it with dung and gravel and piling it into the wooden log shutters that formed the rebuilt wall. Behind the Forever Man stood The Ten, on horseback and fully armed.

Tad rode up next to him.

'Should I rally the men?' he asked. Nathaniel shook his head.

'No. We can deal with this without them.'

'What if they decide to attack?'

Again, the Marine shook his head. 'They won't. There are over five hundred soldiers here. They wouldn't fancy their chances. I reckon that they're here to parley.'

'I wouldn't bet my life on that,' argued Tad. 'They don't see us as much competition. You remember how tough the bastards are. It took all that you had to bring one down. There's fifty of them. And goblins with longbows.'

Nate smiled. 'True, but we have The Ten.'

'Yep, and they have the seventy-five.'

Nate patted Tad on the shoulder. 'Trust me, my friend. They won't attack and if they do then we shall kill them. No more arguments.'

Tad nodded in acceptance then rode amongst the men to tell them to continue working. Then he called the rest of The Ten up to rank alongside him and The Forever Man.

They waited for just over an hour and, when the Orc battle group was about a hundred yards away, Nathaniel kicked his horse into a fast walk and The Ten followed him, arrayed in an arrowhead formation, five on each side. They stopped in front of the battle group.

'Greetings,' said Nathaniel.

'Greetings to you, human,' answered the Orc. 'I am Sergeant Neb,' he continued, pointing to the tattoos of rank on his face.

'I am Nathaniel Degeo Arnthor Hogan, Marine Sergeant, King of the Picts and leader of the New Free State. I am The Forever Man.'

The Orc nodded. 'I have heard of you.'

'How?'

'The wind tells tales of more than the weather,' said the Orc. 'And some beings create their own storms. Nevertheless, King that was, I have been sent to enquire as to what you and your men are doing here?'

'We are refurbishing an ancient artifact in remembrance of our ancestors. It's a cultural thing.'

Sergeant Neb shook his head. 'No,

you are creating a fortified wall across the entire country. And you are doing this without permission.

'Not true,' answered Nathaniel. 'I do have permission.'

'Show me your permit,' demanded the Orc.

'I don't need a permit,' said Nathaniel. 'But take my word for it. I got permission from the leader of the New Free State and he got permission from the people of the New Free State so—I have all the permission that I need.'

'But you are the leader of the New Free State,' pointed out the Orc.

'True,' agreed Nathaniel.

'No,' the Orc shook his head. 'You do not have permission from the Fair-Folk nor do you have permission from a worthy human … therefore, you do not have permission.'

The Marine raised an eyebrow. 'Fine. Okay, you got me. So—stop us.'

'What?'

'Stop us,' repeated Nathaniel.

Orcs are not capable of human expressions. And even if they were there is no way that Sergeant Neb would have felt worry. But he did, somehow, manage to look perturbed.

'Stop what you are doing,' he commanded.

'Go bite yourself,' said Nathaniel and eased his horse forward a couple of steps. The Ten followed him.

In the background the Marine heard the sound of hundreds of clicks of wood striking wood and, when he glanced back over his shoulder he saw that his men had disobeyed him, and they stood ranked along the wall. Five hundred of them with four-foot, steel-tipped wooden arrows fitted to their woomeras.

He smiled.

'Time to go,' he said to the Orc, his voice a low growl. 'And tell your little gray masters, they are not welcome here. This is The New Free State and it is for humans only.'

The Orc sergeant turned around and walked away. His battle group wheeled on the spot and followed him.

Tad let out an audible breath. Nate turned to him and laughed. 'Told you they wouldn't attack.'

Tad chuckled weakly. 'That you did. But they will be back.'

The Marine nodded his agreement.

'Oh yes, and the next time it won't be one crappy little battle group. It'll be the whole outhouse full of them.'

CHAPTER 29

Nathaniel held the tiny piece of gold between his thumb and forefinger, rubbing it softly. It felt slightly soapy, so light as to have no discernable weight. Slightly smaller than his thumbnail and as thick as six sheets of paper held together.

The sunlight drifted through the window and reflected off the buttery surface of the coin. On the one side a figure eight representing the Infinity Symbol and on the reverse "The New Free State."

'How did you do it?' asked Nathaniel.

'Simply,' answered Roo. 'Melted the gold down, spread it onto a flat iron to harden, then used a hammer, anvil, and a die to punch out the coins. That's how I got the milled sides. Then all the left over gets re-melted and we do over. Same with the silver and the copper. They're all the same size, so one gold equals ten silver and one hundred copper. Ergo, we got currency.'

'But how will everyone decide what costs what?' asked Tad.

'Let the market decide. We start by paying the army in coins. Soldiers get ten coppers a day, however, we only physically pay them five. We charge them one copper per meal, three per day, and two coppers for lodging. We don't do this to save coppers, we do it so that they have a base against which to rate their pay. Sergeants get fifteen and captains, twenty.'

'Good thinking, Roo,' encouraged Nathaniel. 'When can you start?'

'Couple of weeks,' answered Roo. 'Got a lot of melting and striking to do.'

There was a knock on the door. 'Come,' said Nathaniel.

A soldier opened the door. 'Sir,' he addressed the Marine. 'I think that you better see this.'

Nathaniel nodded, grabbed his axe, and followed the soldier outside, followed by Tad and Roo.

The soldier pointed.

Across the plains, their bright colors standing out like artworks against the snow, was a train of gaily painted wagons. But not just a few wagons—they stretched back to the horizon.

Nathaniel shaded his eyes and stared, counting in his head.

'Must be at least four hundred of them,' he said.

'And then some,' added Tad. Then he pointed. 'Look.'

A rider had detached himself and was galloping towards them, dark hair flowing back as he rode.

'It's Papa Dante,' said Nate. 'Let him come,' he shouted to the sentries who had drawn their swords.

Papa galloped into the camp and down the main street, stopping in front of Nate. He jumped off his horse and threw his arms around the Marine.

'Greetings, friend,' he bellowed, only slightly breathless from his hard ride. 'I have come, and I have brought reinforcements. Many reinforcements. We have come to join you.' He went down on one knee. 'If you will have us, King Degeo.'

Nathaniel was about to tell Papa to get up but then he realized the seriousness of the walking man's question. He saw that this was a time for pomp and ceremony. A time to bring back some of the old ways. The Pictish ways.

He drew his axe and held the blade out to Papa.

'I shall accept you, Papa Dante. And we shall accept your people. They shall be lauded and applauded in this, The New Free State. Land shall be given them, and they shall be of the free.'

Papa Dante kissed the axe blade.

'Now rise,' said the Marine. 'And from here on you shall be known as Papa Dante, advisor to The Forever Man.'

Papa stood and beamed, his pride and happiness broadly apparent.

'My King.'

Nathaniel grasped him by the shoulder. 'My friend.'

CHAPTER 30

For the first time ever, three humans were invited to sit with the Fair-Folk council of twelve.

Jacob Stone, ranking officer of the horse brigade, in charge of fast messenger services and scouting. A girl from the area called The Farm who went by the name of Milly Human, a surname that she had adopted as she could not remember her actual name. She was there due to her fanatical support and belief in the Fair-Folk and their laws. And, finally, Harry Stand, head of the Society of Worthy Humans, a small quiet man whose physical size belied the magnitude of his ambition.

The reason that commander Ammon Set-Bat had taken this radical step was due mainly to the fact that the humans had declared a New Free State north of the structure known as Hadrian's Wall.

And, only a week or so ago, Orc Sergeant Neb had arrived back at the capital with news that the humans were reinforcing the wall and they had formed an army. He was not sure how large the army was, or indeed even if they were actually trained troops as opposed to simple farmers with spears.

On top of that, Sergeant Neb claimed that, when he had approached the human leader and told him to desist, the thin skin both ignored and insulted the sergeant. This alone was a capital offence, but the sergeant had claimed to have been outnumbered and, rather than suffer a humiliating defeat, he had returned to the capital to report.

So, the council of twelve, Fair-Folk commanders, mages, and merchants—plus the three humans—had met. They had discussed the formation of the New Free State at length and it came to light that Milly Human had actually met the leader of the New Free State, a man called Hogan. Apparently, an ex-warrior from the time before human society had regressed. She also had some complicated, and frankly unbelievable, story regarding his apparent age and where he had been for the last twenty years.

But Seth had used his powers to assess her thought process and, although the human mind was still very much a mystery to him, it was obvious that the girl had mental problems. She had been violently abused at a young age, both her parents had died in front of her, she had come close to starving to death and she blamed both humanity as a whole and Hogan in particular for all of her ills.

Nevertheless, her advice was the same as the other two humans. If order was to be kept, then this threat in the north must be quelled. If not, they predicted that more humans would rally to the banner of the New Free State. And they had also agreed that the operation to put down the rebellion should be swift and overwhelming.

Commander Ammon had agreed but for one point. He did not want to put too many troops into the field. To do so would provide validity to the power of the rebellion, he said. Better to handpick the very best battle groups and attack with the minimum of necessary numbers.

The only problem was, they had no real idea on the actual number of the rebels.

So, he had commanded Seth Hil-Nu, premier mage of the Fair-Folk, to spirit-travel to the north and to obtain some reliable intelligence.

And so, it came to pass that, while his body lay on a cot in his London quarters, the spirit of Seth Hil-Nu was astral traveling, at vast speed, through the firmament.

Heading for Hadrian's Wall.

Below him the landscape peeled away faster than a falcon could fly. Rivers, villages, and forests. Finally, the wall hove into view. But something strange was happening. Although his visibility all around him was one hundred percent, when he tried to see beyond the wall, all was a blur. As if he was trying to see through tears.

Then his forward momentum started to slow. He pushed harder but to no avail. It was like running through quicksand. By the time he got to the wall he could move forward no more, and he hovered in the air in front of the landmark. If he glanced behind himself, he could see to the horizon, but try as he might, when he looked to the north all was covered in a haze.

And then a figure coalesced out of the mist. An old human woman floated in front of him. She wore a long black dress, edged in black lace. Her head was bare. Around her neck a silver chain holding a milky crystal orb. Her eyes were as white and unseeing as the orb on the necklace. Seth could sense the power in her. But he was not afraid, for it was not the power of a warrior; it was, instead, the power of a protector. A healer. Nevertheless, it was powerful enough to be worthy of respect, if not fear.

She held up her hand. 'Leave,' she said.

'No,' answered Seth. 'I have been commanded here and I have a task to complete. It would be remiss of me to leave prior to completion.'

'Regardless,' continued the old woman. 'You should leave for you will be unable to complete your mission.'

'I think not, old one,' said Seth as he gathered his strength, pulling in great gobs of it from the solar flares, inhaling it until he felt that his very soul would explode.

And then he pushed at her barrier with all of his might.

The old woman smiled.

'Typical male,' she said. Her voice a mixture of amusement and pity. 'At the first sign of resistance, use force.'

Seth Hil-Nu was surprised. Amongst the Fair-Folk he was the chief mage. And even if one looked far back into their history one had to go as far as Roth Han-Nu before one found record of a more powerful mage. But this old human hadn't even flinched as he had turned the full weight of his power on her. To her he was less than a child. This, plus the fact that he had never come across a human with the power, was more than annoying.

He felt anger rise within him. The feeling was so strange as to be almost unique. The Fair-Folk prided themselves in their ability to ignore emotions. In fact, they had become so good at doing so that many had completely forgotten what emotions actually were, as well as the power that they were capable of invoking.

Seth pulled in more power and, in a fit of pique, he cast a white-hot fire-ball at the old lady. The ball of plasma pierced the slow area that he could not pass through and struck the old lady in the chest. For a moment flames engulfed her and then, slowly, they flickered out. She looked unharmed but there were definite lines of pain etched across her face.

'Your anger can pierce the veil,' she said. 'But neither you nor your sight may pass.'

She disappeared.

Seth howled in anguish and turned for

home.

CHAPTER 31

'Gogo has ensured the veil of secrecy that she placed in the wall is intact,' assured Papa Dante. 'Apparently one of the gray men attempted to pierce it this afternoon but she held him back. He took a few potshots at her but she's a tough old buzzard, so I'm sure that she'll be okay.'

'I'll go and visit her after this meeting,' said Nathaniel.

Papa nodded. 'She would like that. Now, my King,' continued Papa. 'Discussion needs to be made about the use of my people. As you know, we have formed a semi-permanent encampment of three tabors a few miles down the river. Now my people are free to serve. I have got the women helping in the communal kitchens. The children collect wood and kindling and keep the fires going. But most importantly, I have two hundred fighting men. Now, my King, these are not men to be used on the wall or charging across fields like some sort of blunt weapon. These men are stilettos. Finely honed from years of bushcraft and tough living. I suggest that we break them down into groups of ten. Each group will be known as a zece, our traditional name for a small fighting group. Use them for reconnaissance, guerilla tactics, sabotage, night attacks, that sort of thing. They will not let you down.'

'Thank you, Papa,' acknowledged the Marine. 'Please do it.' He stood up. 'Now I must see Gogo.'

Papa went his way, to see Roo about weapons. Nathaniel mounted his horse and rode to Gogo's vardo.

It took the Marine a few minutes and when he got there he dismounted, ground-haltered his mount, knocked, and let himself in.

Gogo already had a drink waiting for him. She always seemed to know where he was.

She gestured towards the seat opposite her. 'Sit,' she said.

Nathaniel sat and took a sip of the drink. Brandy.

'I hear that you had a run-in with one of the gray men,' he said.

Gogo nodded. 'He was strong but could not find his way through the veil. Their knowledge of magik is great but they are not at one with the earth. They are takers, not nurturers.'

'So, will their sorcerers be a problem?' asked the Marine.

Again, the old lady nodded. 'He pierced my veil with fire. And he did it with ease. My magiks are not created to withstand anger, only prying eyes.'

'So what?' argued Nathaniel. 'Even if they shoot balls of fire at us they'll be doing it blind. Shouldn't be a problem.'

'It will be a problem,' said Gogo. 'I don't know how many adepts they have, but I am assuming hundreds. Imagine thousands of white-hot, explosive balls of fire tumbling from the sky. It would be like world war two carpet-bombing. Not accurate but still deadly.'

Nathaniel sighed. 'What do you suggest that we do, Gogo?'

'I have some people with talent,' she said. 'Mainly women, some young boys. I'd say twenty in all. I will train them, teach them to erect a hard shield. It may work, it may not. Ultimately, Forever Man, it will be up to you to fight magik with magik. So be prepared.'

The Marine toasted her with his glass of brandy. 'I'm always prepared, Gogo,' he said. 'Always.'

***

Milly rode hard, pushing her horse late into the night and stopping only for a brief sleep at whatever inn she was near. Then she would rise early and ride again.

She had to warn Nathaniel. She had to

tell him. He needed to run, to escape into the Scottish Highlands before the Fair-Folk arrived. Because there was no way that he and his rag-tag resistance could hope to stand against the might that was being sent against them.

And it was all her fault. She had regaled commander Ammon. She had argued and disagreed. It was no good, she had told him, to send just enough troops to quash the rebels. What if they lost? What if it was a pyrrhic victory, so close as to remain in dispute?

And then she had told him of humankind and their inherent stubbornness. She had spoken to him of all the legends that she had been told, of Sparta and the three hundred who stood against countless thousands. The battle of Agincourt where King Henry V led a handful of English soldiers against over fifty thousand French and won the battle. The Battle of Britain where the British air force was victorious against overwhelming odds.

And she told him all that she knew of

the American Marines and their Esprit de Corps. The world's largest contingent of special force soldiers, unbowed and unbeaten in battle. Men who lived to fight. Men such as Master Sergeant Nathaniel Hogan. Beware, she had said. For you have not yet come up against a determined human host. Mankind has been bred for war. In its entire recorded history there has never been a moment of worldwide peace—we are always at war.

She had convinced him.

'What do you suggest?' he had asked. And she had told him.

'Use overwhelming force. Send your Orcs and your goblins and your trolls and your mages. Send them in their thousands, for that is the only way that you will win.'

And, in saying thus she had condemned Nathaniel to death. The man who had saved her when her parents had died, the man who had fed her and protected her. Her savior.

The man who had left her to starve and to be raped. God how she hated him.

And now she rode as hard as she could to warn him.

CHAPTER 32

Milly sat bolt upright in her chair, her head high and her eyes clear. But her hands betrayed her as she intertwined her fingers nervously, threading one over the other and then switching her grip over and over.

Finally, Gogo spoke.

'She talks the truth,' she said. 'The Fair-Folk are coming. She is confused, but she is not a liar.'

'I don't understand,' said Tad. 'Why warn us? From what you say, a lot of this is actually your fault.'

'Leave her, Tad,' said Gogo. 'It is sufficient to know that, within days, we shall be attacked in force.' The old blind lady stood up and held her hand out to Milly. 'Now come with me, child,' she said. 'You and I need to have a long talk.'

Milly rose without question and followed Gogo from the room. She avoided the Marine's eyes.

Nathaniel spoke for the first time. 'Roo, how goes construction on the wall?'

'As well as can be expected, Chief,' answered the Aussie. 'But we can't man the whole thing. We simply don't have enough men.'

Nathaniel shook his head. 'We won't need to. The Fair-Folk are looking to stamp us out. They aren't looking to occupy the New Free State. What would be the point? It would just turn into an endless mêlée of guerilla warfare. No, wherever we stand, they will come to.'

'Well then, Chief,' said Roo. 'The wall right here is the best point. We have the fortress behind us, a twenty-foot wall in front, fairly level land without trees or mountains to conceal the approach. The only problem is, they could simply outflank us and attack from the back, as well as the front. Could cause problems.'

Nathaniel opened a desk drawer and

pulled out a map that he unfolded and laid on the desk.

'Look here.' He pointed. 'This is where they will come; it's the most direct route from London. They know where we are; their mages will be able to discern that much. Now, this is what I propose. Firstly, Roo, you take five thousand men and dig two trenches that run at right angles to the wall.' The Marine grabbed a pencil and drew on the map. 'Here and here. A thousand yards apart and two thousand yards long. I want it at least twelve-foot-wide and ten foot deep. Line the side with the spoil so that it's even deeper. Then erect wooden stakes at the bottom. Also litter them with caltrops.'

Roo looked at the map. The two trenches ran parallel to each other, away from the wall like the two arms of a giant U with the wall at the bottom of it.

Nathaniel continued. 'Then I will place the cavalry in the hills here, and here.' He pointed at areas outside of the arms of the U. 'Also, Papa Dante and his boys will be roving the surrounding area.

This will ensure that, once committed, the Fair-Folk attack will be centered on this section of the wall. There will be no way to outflank us. The battle will begin and end here.' He stabbed the map with the pencil. 'Right, gentlemen, we need to ready the troops. Tad, tell Paul Brighton where to place his cavalry. After that, organize arrows, rocks, and spears to be stockpiled along the wall. Also, water butts and fire braziers. Tad, when you speak to Brighton tell him to send scouts out beyond the wall. We need as much warning as we can get. Move it, our survival depends on a certain amount of speed.'

Nathaniel sat alone in the room. Outside were ten thousand souls. They were there because of him and him alone. And, in the next few days, they would be facing an alien race in hand-to-hand combat for their lives. Not only their lives but also for the future freedom of the human race.

What gave him the right to decide on the fate of humanity?

The Marine scrubbed his eyes with the butt of his hands. They were dry, and they stung as if lemon juice had been poured into them.

Was the loss of freedom too high a price to pay for lawfulness and safety?

What if they lost? What if they won? Nathaniel stood up.

He was a Marine. He was a king. He was a sergeant. He was a rifleman. He was a time traveler. He was an axeman. He was an immortal.

He was … The Forever Man.

Nathaniel pushed his axe into his belt and strode from the room heading to the wall. It was time to talk to his men.

Time to lead.

CHAPTER 33

It had taken the host six days to arrive. The night before, they had camped out of bowshot, their campfires as numerous as stars in the sky.

Then, that morning, while the mist still covered the ground with its gossamer breath, they formed up. Rank upon rank of Orcs in full battle gear. They stood shield to shield, one thousand bodies wide and fifteen deep. Behind them were the massed blocks of the goblin archers, ten thousand strong.

Between the Orcs and the goblins stood a rank of massive hairy creatures, ten feet tall carrying huge shields and long broad spears—the trolls.

To the right-hand side of the archers, a pavilion had been erected and, standing on the wall and using a pair of old Zeiss binoculars, Nathaniel could see the Fair-Folk. At least six of them, seated around a table, sipping from goblets, and eating dainties. A pair of goblin horn blowers also stood on the pavilion, waiting for orders.

'I reckon slightly over twenty-five thousand of them,' said Roo.

The Marine nodded. 'At least.'

'We're screwed then, aren't we?' questioned the Aussie.

Nathaniel laughed. 'Looking on the bright side, I see. That's what I love about you, Roo. Your never-ending optimism.'

Roo grimaced. 'Only being realistic, Chief,' he said. 'We're outnumbered over two to one, not great odds.'

'Not great,' agreed Nathaniel. 'We've got Papa Dante and two thousand cavalry hidden in the hills on each side of them. I've sent two thousand of our men back to guard the closest villages in case it all goes badly for us, and we have six thousand on the wall. So actually, it's closer to four to one odds.'

Roo spat on the floor. 'Told you. We're screwed.'

Nathaniel patted Roo on the shoulder. 'Take heart, my friend, for none of them are men such as us. We can, and we will, win this.'

The Marine handed the binoculars back to Roo. 'Time to talk to the boys. It won't be long now.'

And The Forever Man walked down the length of the wall. Stopping and chatting to individual soldiers. Laughing with some, cajoling others. Strengthening them with a word, a touch, a look.

When he got to the end of the wall he walked back and stopped in the middle. He had split The Ten into three groups. Four stood with him and three on each end of the wall. They were the best of the best and he hoped that they would help to boost morale to all around them.

As the sun burned away the last tendrils of mist, the Orc battle drums sounded. A solid rhythmic marching beat.

And the host started forward.

Nathaniel cast out his orb of light and drew in some power. Enough so that, when he spoke, his voice would carry to all on the wall.

'Here they come, boys,' he said, keeping his voice conversational, allowing the magik to amplify it. 'No need for speeches, we all know why we're here. Steady now, there are enough of them for all of us. Steady.'

The host tramped closer, the massive horny feet of the Orcs smashing into the ground in unison, the trolls shambling amongst them and the goblins marching behind with lighter step. Nathaniel noticed that many of the Orcs were carrying scaling ladders for the wall.

The ground throbbed in time to the march like a gigantic heartbeat.

And then Nathaniel felt the hair on his arms and neck rise. Like a great wave of static electricity had washed over him. At the same time, he heard a high-pitched shriek, right at the edge of his hearing.

'Can you feel that?' he asked Tad. 'And that noise, can you hear it?'

Tad shook his head. 'Sorry, Chief. All that I can hear is the stomping of those bloody great Orc feet.'

Without warning a series of white-hot flaming balls of plasma launched from the Fair-Folk pavilion and streaked towards the wall, heading straight for Nathaniel.

There was a collective groan from the men as they watched the fireballs coming, helpless to do anything about it.

But, twenty yards out from the wall they exploded, as if they had struck an invisible barrier.

Nathaniel punched the air. 'Oorah!' he shouted. 'Gogo and her acolytes rule.'

A cheer went up from the men as they realized that they were protected from the Fair-Folk magik. Nathaniel only wished that they could have also protected against arrows and spears, but Gogo had said that magik could only protect against magik. Shields and armor would have to do against standard weapons.

'Right, boys,' said the Marine in his magik-enhanced voice. 'Now it's our turn. Lock and load, missiles ready.' There was the sound of six thousand wooden clicks as the Free Men loaded their arrows into their woomeras. 'Fire!'

Six thousand heavy arrows fluted into the air. 'Reload,' shouted the Marine. 'Fire. Reload … fire. Reload … fire. Reload … fire.'

By the time the first six thousand arrows struck there were already another eighteen thousand in the air.

The Orcs raised their shields above their heads and the arrows struck with sound like hail on a tin roof.

Most of the arrows bounced off shields and helms and armor. But some found flesh. Unprotected necks, faces, and feet. Orcs went down but, as they did, the row behind would move up to take their place. Moving forward. Implacable. Emotionless. Like a well-oiled machine.

Then the goblin archers were in range. Ten thousand bows bent and fired. Ten thousand cloth-yard steel-tipped arrows flew into the air. Again, and again, and again.

'Shields!' shouted Nathaniel.

The men grabbed their shields and held them above their heads. Arrows whispered down from the heavens. As thick as a rainstorm. As powerful as a tsunami. The screams of the wounded and dying rent the air as steel tore through flesh and bone.

And then they were there.

Ladders thrown up against the wall. Orcs swarming up in their hundreds, climbing onto the wall.

'Repel them,' shouted Nathaniel. 'Repel the bastards.' A face appeared in front of him. Gray, half covered with a bronze helmet. Piggy eyes. No nose. Nathaniel swung his axe and shattered the thing's skull. It fell backwards without a sound only to be replaced by another. He swung again, the axe dancing in his grip like a living thing. An extension of his own limbs. A steel-bladed extra arm.

All along the wall men hacked and hewed. Grunting with the effort as they swung their heavy swords, their axes, and their spears.

Next to him Tad was wreaking havoc with his two long knives. One in each hand, he would stab viciously at the eyes of any pig-face that breached the wall, jumping back and forth, as graceful as a dancer as he danced the death salsa.

The sound of steel on steel slowed and then stopped and Nathaniel realized that the Orcs were retreating. Not one had made it on to the top of the wall.

He heard the sound of whispering death as the ten thousand goblins unleashed their arrows once again.

'Shields!' he shouted.

And his men raised their shields above their heads for a second time in order to weather the storm of steel death.

'Return fire,' commanded the Marine. 'We can outrange them with our woomeras. Get up, get up.' He stood up and walked along the wall, arrows whispering all around him. One clanged off his chest plate, leaving a bright scratch mark. 'Come on, boys. Show them what we're made of.'

The men stood up and fitted the heavy arrows to their woomeras. Goblin arrows struck human flesh and many men went down. But then the human arrows were in flight and they descended on the goblins like the very wrath of the gods themselves. The heavy oak and steel bolts punching into the lightly armored archers, shattering helms, riveting them to the ground. Sometimes literally splitting them in half as they smashed into them.

Unable to withstand the onslaught, the goblins withdrew out of range and their weapons lay silent.

A cheer went up amongst the humans. 'Oorah!'

'Clear the walls,' commanded Nathaniel. 'Look to the wounded. Don't throw the ladders down, pick them up and put them down on our side so they can't use them again. Come on, boys.'

Roo came running up, behind him were a bunch of young boys, Papa Dante's people. Some were carrying stretchers, others mugs, and water barrels.

Nathaniel nodded at the Aussie. 'Thanks, Roo. Good thinking.'

And all around, the Free Men cleared up and treated their wounded, restocked the supplies of arrows, replaced rent shields and shattered swords, and quenched their thirsts.

An hour later the Orcs came again.

***

Someone handed Nathaniel a chunk of bread and a lump of cheese. He chewed on it mechanically, washing it down with water from a jug.

The Orcs had come three more times that day and the Marine was exhausted beyond belief. But his unbelievable skill with the axe and his ability to move faster than any normal human had motivated his own men to perform at a higher level than would normally have been possible. He was a god of war and they were his disciples.

On the third attack the Orcs had managed to make it onto the wall, coming over the top in two separate places. But in both instances The Forever Man had used his freakish speed and strength to beat them back. His massive, two-bladed axe cleaving flesh and bone as he hacked them down.

By the time the sun was setting, men had to spread river sand on the battlements to stop slipping on the congealing blood that the walkways were awash with.

Nathaniel had overtaxed himself. He had written checks that his body was now unable to cash. Even the act of breathing was proving almost too much for him. Tad had sent for Gogo and the old lady had arrived, taken a quick look at The Forever Man, and then brewed up an herbal tisane for him and made him drink the whole pot. Color had returned to his cheeks and now, finally, he was able to eat, albeit without any enjoyment or even acknowledgement of what he was doing.

Gogo pulled Tad aside.

'Watch him, little big man,' she had said. 'Make sure that he sleeps and tomorrow, when they come again, ensure that The Ten are with him. Another day of such expenditure of energy may leech his life force from him. Today he did the work of twenty men. If he does the same tomorrow I doubt that he will survive.'

'But, I thought that he was immortal,' argued Tad. 'Oh, he will not die,' said Gogo. 'But his life force will be extinguished. He will live out eternity as a mere shell. A vegetable. Forever.'

Tad shuddered at the thought. 'I'll take care of him, Gogo.'

She patted Tad on the cheek and walked away. That night Nathaniel slept like the dead.

He woke in the morning before sunrise. Bright and full of energy, no trace of the prior day's exhaustion.

Tad breathed a sigh of relief.

'So, little big man,' said Nathaniel. 'How did we fare yesterday?'

'Lost almost a thousand men dead or injured. I'd say we took out two thousand of them, maybe more,' said Tad. 'Another two days like that and it's all over. We can't hold the wall with less than three thousand men.'

'Don't worry,' said the Marine. 'I've been in these extended battles before. I saw it when I fought amongst the Picts. Today we won't lose nearly as many. The gods of war are annealing us, cutting the fat. The ones that we lost were our weakest, slowest, least lucky. Brave men, make no mistake, but the weakest go first. Harsh but true. You shall see today, we won't lose more than two or three hundred.'

Nathaniel felt the surge of static electricity again and a high-pitched roaring in his ears. He pulled in some power and pulsed a thought at Gogo.

'Gogo, can you hear me?'

'Yes, child.' Gogo's reply echoed softly in his skull. 'No need to shout. Simply think and I shall hear.'

'Something's happening,' thought Nathaniel. 'Their mages are going to attack. It feels different to yesterday though. Harder, more powerful.'

'We are ready,' reassured Gogo. 'Do not worry.'

The noise in Nathaniel's ears reached a crescendo, but when he looked around him it was obvious that no one else could hear it. Then, lightning started to march across the open ground towards them. Each blinding detonation getting closer. Pillars of exploding incandescent white light. But, like the fireballs, when they reached the twenty-yard mark they simply skittered and smashed away at the invisible screen and then faded out.

The men cheered and stuck their fingers up at the enemy, cursing and insulting them.

Then the war drums started again, and thirteen thousand Orcs tramped towards the wall.

As they had the day before, the men unleashed their heavy arrows and the goblins replied with their cloth-yards. The Orcs reached the wall and threw up their scaling ladders and the battle truly began.

The Marine strode the battlements like a force of nature. His axe swung without pause, hacking, dismembering. Killing. Heat boiled off him in waves and his black armor became red with the dark essence of the Orcs.

And men died in their hundreds. And Orcs died in their thousands.

Again, they came. And again.

On their fourth charge they broached the top of the wall, forming a square on the right-hand side. Nathaniel cried out and forged towards them, his axe held high.

They were as wheat before the scythe. Chaff before the storm.

Tad stood back and watched in awe. It wasn't only the Marine's superior speed, or his strength. It was the fact that he deigned not to defend himself. The double-bladed axe was all about attack. There was no subtlety in movement. There was grace and skill, a dance was being performed, but it was simple dance. A crude two- step without grace nor rhythm. It was simple momentum. The heartbeat of the storm. The elegance of an avalanche. A poetry of destruction. And it caught others up in its maelstrom, dragging them into its vortex of violence, empowering all around him as they saw their king wreak havoc on the enemy.

And behind him strode The Ten, their blood-red armor glistening in the wan sunlight, their massive broadswords cleaving all before. A combine harvester of death.

There were many casualties, for the Orcs were bred for battle and they were tough and resilient.

But they were not human. They were not men.

So, when the sun crept back behind the horizon, leaving the dark to cover the devastation and ruin with its cloak of night, the wall was still under the sole occupancy of the Free Men.

***

Torches guttered and spat on the wall as the sentries peered into the night. Nathaniel had left guards on the wall although he was sure that the Orcs would not attack during the night. It would have held no advantage for them.

Now he walked amongst the wounded. Rows and rows of them in makeshift tents. He had been wrong when he had told Tad that their losses would be limited to a couple of hundred that day. They had, in fact, lost another five hundred dead or injured. And the cries of the wounded wrung at his heart.

But none complained to him as he greeted them. Stopping to kneel next to them and holding their hands. Encouraging them. Praising their courage.

They smiled as best they could. Some winked at him, others saluted from their bloody beds. Others were too gravely injured to move, but their pain-filled eyes followed him as he passed, and in them he saw no blame, only pride, honor.

Suddenly he felt his hair rise and heard a keening in his ears.

'Gogo,' he pulsed a mental shout. There was no answer. 'Gogo!' he screamed again.

Finally, she answered. Her mental voice quiet and sleep filled.

'Yes, child. What is it?'

'They're attacking. The Fair-Folk are attacking. Something's coming.'

'There's no time for me to wake the acolytes,' said Gogo. 'You must throw up a shield. Do it. Now.'

'How?' asked the Marine.

But there was no answer and, anyway, it was too late. Lightning marched through the camp, stabbing blindly at the earth with large blue-white daggers of explosive heat. The wounded flew into the air, their bedclothes burning, their flesh sloughing off them in slabs. Tents caught alight and men that were struck directly simply exploded.

Nathaniel drew in power and then pushed back. He had no idea what he was doing. He simply reacted, fighting power with yet more power. The air above the wall literally burst into flame. Gouts of yellow fire poured down onto the wall and the plains beyond, burning men and Orcs alike. Nathaniel had absolutely no control over his power and the firestorm cascaded from side to side. Vast areas of forest burst into flame. Pillars of fire shot high into the atmosphere, lighting up the very clouds themselves with a sickly sodium-yellow glow.

The Fair-Folk pavilion burst into flame sending its occupants scurrying away in panic.

Nathaniel collapsed to the floor in a dead faint and the firestorm switched off instantly, leaving only burning grass, smoldering timbers, and the rank steaming bodies of fire-killed Orcs and humans alike.

Gogo appeared out of the smoke and wreckage, blind but all-seeing. She walked straight up to the Marine and knelt next to him. She slapped his cheeks a few times and he came to, shaking his head groggily.

'Messy,' she said to him. 'No control. Still, they appear to have stopped.'

Tad came running up.

'What the hell was that?' he shouted.

'The Fair-Folk attacked us,' replied Gogo. 'Nathaniel here reacted to stop them.'

'So, the fire storm?' enquired Tad.

Gogo nodded. 'Yes, that was he.'

'Wow!' exclaimed the little big man. 'Talk about collateral damage. Still, I see that he sorted their pavilion out. Now the gray men have got to grovel in the mud like the rest of their troops.'

Gogo stood up. 'Get him something to eat, he'll be fine. Make sure he rests tonight. Tomorrow will be another long day.'

Gogo left, going back to her vardo while, all around her, Roo and his assistants separated the dead from the dying, put out fires and tried to bring some semblance of order to the chaos.

The next morning the Orcs came early, appearing out of the fading dark, dragging tendrils of mist with them. Eleven thousand strong with three thousand archers. Their numbers substantially depleted but still they outnumbered the humans more than three to one.

This day was different to the preceding two. There were no battle cries. No shouted insults. Man and Orc fought in silence save for grunts of effort and the odd dying scream.

All energy was channeled into killing. Destroying. Ending.

There was bravery. A man, stabbed through the gut, running into an Orc, grabbing him, and forcing him off the wall, taking three others with him as he fell down the scaling ladder. Another man, jumping in front of an Orc's blade meant for a friend, taking the steel in his chest, and smiling, knowing that he had saved his comrade's life.

There was cowardice. A man dropping his blade and running from the wall, ignoring the calls for help, leaving his compatriots to die.

There was sadness. A young man, sitting on the wall, his entrails spilling out of his stomach, falling between his fingers as he cried for his mother.

There was vengeance. The Forever Man, striding the walls like a colossus. His axe the forbearer of death. And the Orcs shrank back before him and squealed in porcine terror as he bore down on them.

And, finally, the host broke and retreated once again. Nathaniel climbed down from the wall and Roo met him with a jug of water. The Marine drank thirstily and then poured the rest over himself, washing the blood from his face and neck, rinsing the deep viscous redness from his hair and beard.

'Chief,' said Roo. 'Slight problem.'

'What?' asked Nathaniel.

Roo pointed behind him. Standing there, arrayed in neat battle formation, were the two thousand men that Nathaniel had sent to guard the villages in case the Orcs got past the wall.

'They said that they would stand no longer. They said that their place is beside their king. So, they came. I couldn't stop them.'

Nathaniel walked up to one of the captains who stood in the front of the ranks.

'You. Captain Harlow, isn't it?'

The man nodded, a slight sheen of nervous sweat on his face.

'So, Harlow,' continued Nathaniel. 'You deign to disobey a direct command from me?'

Harlow shook his head. 'No, sir. Definitely not, sir. Possible misunderstanding, sir.'

'Misunderstanding?'

Harlow nodded. 'Yes, sir. We have checked the villages and there is no immediate problem, so we returned here, sir.'

Nathaniel smiled. 'Fine then, Captain. We shall settle for that. A misunderstanding. So, you want to fight?'

As one, the men all shouted. 'Oorah!'

'Good,' said the Marine. 'Because I have a plan.' He drew in a little power and pulsed a command to all of the men on the wall. 'Come down. Everyone, form up behind the reinforcements. Do it now.'

There was an instant flurry of activity as captains and sergeants started shouting. Men scurried back and forth, grabbing helms and shields and spears. Twenty minutes later the Free Men stood in neat ranks. Almost seven thousand of them, waiting for Nathaniel's command.

The Marine concentrated and then pulsed a thought to Papa Dante.

'Papa.'

'My King. Is that you?'

'None other. Where are you?'

'We have split into two groups of one hundred. Either side of the host, under cover alongside the trenches.'

'Good, on my command I want you to use your woomeras to target the trolls. I need them down, Papa. After the trolls you can concentrate on the Orc officers. Who is in charge of the other group?'

'Tarquin.'

'Fine,' Nathaniel pulsed the same message to Tarquin who acknowledged.

Then the Marine contacted Brighton and his two-thousand cavalry.

'Brighton.'

'Chief,' he responded. 'You're in my head! How are you doing this?'

'Not important,' answered Nathaniel. 'As long as you can hear me. Now, where are you?'

'The woods, sir. Waiting.'

'Good. On my command, I want you

all to ride hell-for-leather to engage the Orcs. I need you to bottle them up between the two trenches and the wall. Got it?'

'On your command, sir.' Nathaniel turned to face his men.

'People,' he said in his magik-enhanced voice. 'It's speech time. This is where I tell you that we are the last bastion of freedom in a world that has gone to shit. We are the last of the Free Men. The fate of the world blah, blah, blah. Well I don't do speeches. I have one thing to say, so listen up. This ends here. It ends now. I'm sick of the Orcs attacking us. Now it's our turn. So, stay frosty and follow me, it's time to kick pig-faced butt. Oorah!'

'OORAH!'

The Forever Man cast out his bubble of light, letting it caress the land, letting it climb high into the sky, sending it deep into the womb of mother Earth. Then he pulled it slowly back in, bringing with it untold amounts of power. Many times, more than he had ever come close to handling before.

He could feel his muscles tightening and his heart thumping in his chest. His tongue started to swell in his mouth and his eyes started to burn. Then his teeth began to clatter together as the energy overflowed from him. Pain rose in him like a barometer level after a storm and his vision clouded over, the whites of his eyes turning red with broken blood vessels.

And, as he drew more and more power in, the Orcs charged once again, their feet crashing across the plain, coming closer and yet closer.

Then they were almost at the wall.

Nathaniel pointed at the base of the structure and punched the power out.

The wall did not simply explode—it disintegrated. Four thousand tons of gravel, wood, and mortar detonated with a blast equivalent to fifty tons of TNT. Bigger than the biggest conventional bomb that the world possessed prior to the pulse. Over a thousand Orcs and a thousand goblins perished in those first few microseconds as they were pulped by the tons of flying shrapnel.

Nathaniel screamed in pain but unlike before, he didn't pass out. Instead he pulled in power once again and bellowed out a command that all could hear.

'Charge. Everybody—charge! For Freedom!'

Seven thousand Free Men charged across the plain towards the ten thousand Orcs and goblins. On each side of the trenches, Papa Dante's men stood up and fired a stream of arrows at the massive trolls, riddling them with steel-pointed oak.

And the thunder of hooves drowned out all else as two thousand mounted men came galloping from the forest to fall on the host with lance and saber.

Nathaniel saw a gaggle of little gray Fair-Folk running into the forest in an attempt to escape, they had given up using their glamour and were visible as their usual small gray selves. Papa Dante's men cut them down as they ran, piercing their small, rubbery bodies with countless shafts.

The Marine fought with a mindless fury, sweeping his huge battle-axe from side to side, shearing through armor and sword, and flesh and bone.

The cavalry ranged back and forth across the battlefield, standing in their stirrups, and hacking downwards with their long, curved sabers. No quarter was asked nor given.

Ultimately it was the human cavalry that won the day. The Orcs and goblins had never fought against mounted warriors before and they simply had no idea how to protect themselves from an armed man running them down using over one thousand pounds of angry, sharp-hoofed, large-toothed animal.

It was not in the Orcs' breeding to surrender, it simply wasn't an option that they considered. So, after the host's cohesion as a fighting unit had been broken, it became a simple slaughter. The Free Men had to kill every last pig-face and the slaughter went on past sunset.

Then, finally, it was over.

And on that terrible day over fifteen thousand Orcs and goblins died—as did over two thousand Free Men.

The humans worked late into the night, fighting against their own exhaustion as they felled trees and collected the dead, building huge funeral pyres for enemy and human alike.

The next morning saw the sky thick with the gray greasy smoke of the burnings. A final tribute to the brave and the foolhardy, the cowardly and the courageous. The Orcs—and the humans.

Enemies in life, brothers in death.

And Nathaniel wept openly when Tad gave him the numbers of the dead and he ordered a wall of dressed stone to be built and on that wall the name of every Free Man that had perished during those days defending the wall so that they were never forgotten.

EPILOGUE

It had been two months since the great battle of the wall and the scouts had seen no presence of any Orcs within miles ever since.

Roo and a crew of men had rebuilt the destroyed wall and, this time, he had installed a large wooden gate that ran on rollers so that the wall could be opened, and cavalry could sally forth.

One hundred and twenty men died of their wounds in the weeks following the battle and their names were added to the stonewall of remembrance. Three of The Ten had died and Tad had chosen replacements out of the very best of the best of the survivors.

Nathaniel continued to live in the main fortress that was attached to the wall and his quarters were added to and increased. He had a hall built and a large round table installed. Big enough to fit twenty people.

Milly continued to stay with Gogo and the walking folk. Nathaniel asked to see her but Gogo refused him permission. It was not yet time, she told him.

Tad grew worried about Nathaniel. The Marine would rise late and then walk down to the wall of remembrance and simply stare at it for hours on end, reading the names over and over again.

He would eat the food brought to him and drink the water, but he became less and less communicative and the running of the New Free State fell more to Tad, Roo, and Papa Dante.

Then one day, just before lunch, Tad went to The Forever Man.

'Come,' he said. 'There is something that I want you to see.'

Nathaniel followed the little big man as he climbed the stairway to the top of the wall.

'Look,' said Tad, and he pointed.

In the distance he saw them. Hundreds upon hundreds of people. Wagons, push carts, horses. People on foot, herding goats and cows and sheep before them.

And above them flew the black and silver flag of the New Free State.

Humanity had found a place to be free.

The Forever Man smiled and went down onto the plains to welcome his people.

A NOTE FROM THE AUTHOR

Thank you for reading Clan Wars. If you enjoyed it, please leave a review … I know that it's a hassle but us writers rely on your kindhearted input. We need you to help us!

If you would like to discuss anything at all, please email me at zuffs@sky.com—my private email, and we can have a chat.

Keep your eyes open for the next book …
THE FOREVER MAN: Book 4
UNICORN

http://a.co/aGQpidx

53919835R00216

Made in the
USA
Lexington, KY